"What about us?"

"What *about* us?" JJ repeated.

"You've got all of these plans on finding your brother and stopping Lawson," Price said. "You even said you know what you want after it's all done."

JJ nodded.

"But you'll stay here? In Seven Roads?"

She nodded again.

"So, Seven Roads is settled, then. You, this house is where you'll stay?"

"That's the plan."

"You say the words, but... You've convinced yourself that you *need* to keep up the life of JJ Shaw. Of the woman who can hack into websites, fight close combat in elevators, make my kid laugh and fit right into my life without even trying."

JJ didn't move.

"So I'm asking again. What about us? What about me? What do you feel like you need to do if everything works out? And what about if it doesn't? Because I'm not like you, JJ. I know what I want and I know what I need, and it's one and the same."

"And what's that?"

He put his hand against her cheek.

"You."

THE DEPUTY'S
SECRET DOUBLE

TYLER ANNE SNELL

Harlequin

INTRIGUE

This book is for Chelsea M. Without your late-night writing chats, JJ and Price would still be stuck in my head. Thank you. And may you meet your word count always.

ISBN-13: 978-1-335-45736-3

The Deputy's Secret Double

Copyright © 2025 by Tyler Anne Snell

Harlequin Enterprises ULC
22 Adelaide St. West, 41st Floor
Toronto, Ontario M5H 4E3, Canada
www.Harlequin.com

Printed in Lithuania

Recycling programs for this product may not exist in your area.

MIX
Paper | Supporting responsible forestry
FSC® C021394

Tyler Anne Snell lives in South Alabama with her same-named husband, their artist kiddo, four mini "lions" and a burning desire to meet Kurt Russell. Her superpowers include binge-watching TV and herding cats. When she isn't writing thrilling mysteries and romance, she's reading everything she can get her hands on. How she gets through each day starts and ends with a big cup of coffee. Visit her at www.tylerannesnell.com.

Books by Tyler Anne Snell

Harlequin Intrigue

Manhunt
Toxin Alert
Dangerous Recall

Small Town Last Stand

Search for the Truth
The Deputy's Secret Double

The Saving Kelby Creek Series

Uncovering Small Town Secrets
Searching for Evidence
Surviving the Truth
Accidental Amnesia
Cold Case Captive
Retracing the Investigation

Visit the Author Profile page at Harlequin.com.

CAST OF CHARACTERS

Perry "Price" Collins—Future plans have always seemed up in the air for this single-father deputy. Yet when he runs into a beautiful woman who will do anything to protect her secret, he finds himself ready to do anything to protect her.

JJ Shaw—Moving to Seven Roads under a new identity to investigate a yearslong family secret was easy enough. Having to team up with a too-trusting and handsome deputy who refuses to let her run into danger alone? That's the hard part.

Winnie Collins—Price's teenage daughter, this kind and smart girl gives both Price and JJ a reason to keep fighting.

Josiah Teller—A young man whose suspicious call and attack starts off a chain reaction that affects JJ and Price's investigations.

The Unknown Brother—The reason why JJ comes to town. The race to find out her biological brother's identity has everyone scrambling.

Rose Little—A friend of Price's, this deputy doesn't let any danger stop her from helping back up the people she cares about.

Lydia Ortiz—As JJ's real identity, her life before Seven Roads is her most guarded secret.

Prologue

By all accounts, JJ Shaw was an all-rounder. There wasn't just one thing she was good at. She flourished at a great many things that left her résumé looking like a run-over garden of skill, determination and a little luck.

She was great at math, was a pro at public speaking, won accolades for leadership, never said no to hard work but also never let anyone use her as a doormat. She was fluent in Spanish, had a steel-trap memory, and had spent several summers at STEM retreats that gave her a leg up in any job setting that revolved around computer software or programming. Her degrees—all three of them—were impressive by themselves, never mind together, and when she wasn't contracting out her services to corporate juggernauts across the country to keep her savings account plump and happy, she spent her free time dominating boxing gyms and specialized training camps in various fields.

JJ Shaw wasn't just well-rounded on paper. She was a delight, a wonder and a laugh and a half in person too.

She wasn't just an all-rounder.

She was *the* all-rounder.

Which made the almost-blank piece of paper she slid across the counter hurt just a little.

"I know I don't have much to offer but I can promise

you I'll work hard," she told the woman standing on the opposite side.

The best JJ could guess was that the owner of Twenty-Two Coffee Shop was only a few years older than her thirty. If that. Her name tag read Cassandra and her eyes read hesitance. Her protruding, pregnant belly read an opposing eagerness.

She glanced at the Part-Time Wanted sign taped to the glass front door before settling on prioritizing her needs over her polite Southern concerns.

"I'm not sure if this type of work is something you'll want," she tried. "It's part-time, as you saw, and that really does mean part-time. It won't pay that much and most of the work is cleaning and helping with back-end things until I come back. We have another part-timer already who works after school and on the weekends and then my sister and another full-timer. This is a position that's more for dealing with the things that fall through the cracks when I'm out on maternity leave."

JJ had once spent an entire summer cleaning out horse stalls and pig pens in the middle of the Alabama heat, morning in and morning out. The smells alone were imprinted in her memory forever and it was one of her least favorite jobs. Keeping a coffee shop in the small Georgia town of Seven Roads seemed a much less offensive situation. At the very least it was air-conditioned.

She smiled.

"I don't mind the work, even if it's low on the hours," she assured her. "Honestly, I'm in need of an excuse to get out and about more than anything. I've just come to town and want to see something other than my own walls. Plus, I'd love to have some extra money coming in from somewhere to feel better about the house I just bought."

JJ could see she had piqued Cassandra's interest.

Seven Roads was thimble-sized small. Everyone truly knew everyone. Or, at least, everyone had *heard* about everyone else. Someone always had all the stories, true or not, about every resident.

Old and new.

JJ had been in Seven Roads for over a month and had been careful to only be seen exactly when she wanted to be seen. This was the first time Cassandra had spoken to her and, as far as both women knew, it was the first time the old home on Whatley Bend had been brought up by the newcomer crazy enough to buy it.

Now it was up to Cassandra to take the bait.

She did, though JJ had to admit she was more even keel about it than she thought others might have been.

"You're the one who bought Janice Wilkins's old home? The one over on Whatley Bend?"

JJ nodded.

"I'm working on a plan to renovate it since it's been in such poor condition. I'm staying in a rental near here until then."

Cassandra was impressed.

"That's a lot of work if I remember that house right. You have a lot cut out for yourself." She glanced at the front door sign again. "I'm not sure you'll have the time to be here if you're doing all that."

JJ was quick with a new smile, quicker with a response.

"I'm just overseeing. I won't be doing the work myself," she said. "Plus, you said the hours here were on the low side. I can more than work around that if you give me the chance."

Under normal circumstances, JJ had the feeling the Cassandra might have wondered more about the situation. Yet, she rubbed a hand along her pregnant belly and sighed.

It sure helped JJ's cause that no one else had applied for the job yet.

Cassandra finally relented with a nod.

"If you really don't mind the low hours and the work, let's see if we can figure something out."

JJ made a show of being overjoyed.

"Thank you. You won't be sorry."

Cassandra pulled her résumé across the counter and then motioned JJ to follow her down the hall to the back. She only paused when the bell over the front door rang, and a teenaged girl called a hello.

"That's our other part-timer," she explained to JJ when they were settled in the manager's office. "Even though her daddy can be overprotective sometimes, she's a hoot to have around. I'm sure you'll end up having a good time when she's on shift."

JJ said she was looking forward to that and then they got down to the business side of hiring someone new. When that was done, Cassandra went on a little about some of the regular customers and commented carefully on a few more.

She didn't know it, but JJ was hanging on her every word as she did so.

Then, when a name she was hoping would be said never came, her attention went back to casual.

It made lying easier when the number one question she had been asked since moving to town came.

"So, Miss Shaw, what brought you to Seven Roads?"

JJ smiled once more.

"My dad stayed here for business years ago and I liked the idea of the slower pace when I was trying to figure out where to go next. Also, I think we all hit that urge sometimes for a change. I've just been lucky enough to be able to find a way to make it happen."

Cassandra accepted the answer with a solemn nod.

"I've been there before, for sure," she said. "Sometimes you need space from the bad to realize all of the good still out there."

It was JJ's turn to nod.

Though she felt the strain in her smile.

She couldn't say it—wouldn't say it—but the life JJ had been living before was the good. It was stressful at times, sure, and there were secrets she couldn't touch, but it had been nice and fun and safe.

Now she was JJ Shaw.

She had left that good and jumped right into a past filled with bad.

There was no normal life left for her now that she was in Seven Roads.

She was only there to do one thing and one thing only.

JJ was there to keep a secret, and no one was going to stop her from doing that.

Chapter One

Perry Price Collins already wasn't having the best of days, way before he took the punch to the jaw.

First, as in as soon as he rolled off the couch, his cell phone was buzzing with the sheriff's caller ID.

"I can't promise this in writing, and it definitely won't hold up in court, but I'll pay you everything in my bank account if you could do me a favor." Instead of Liam Weaver, current sheriff of Seven Roads, his wife, Blake, was on the other end of the line, laughing into her own words. But Price could hear she surely wanted the favor.

He rubbed his eyes, grimaced at the slight hangover already beating at his skull and nodded to his empty room.

"You know, I was just out with your husband a few hours ago. Can't this favor take pity on me and wait until later?"

Blake laughed. Or, really, more like cackled. Since marrying the sheriff, she had become more comfortable with teasing him. And especially when he looped in a poor, unsuspecting Price for a "quick drink." That quick drink was now muddy boots in the living room, a bar tab that he couldn't exactly remember and a hangover that he couldn't ignore if he wanted to.

"If you want sympathy, let me remind you who came and picked you two fools up last night. And who fought with some guy for a solid five minutes because he was sure as sure that his keys were back at the bar when they were in fact in his *hand*."

Price squinted, like it would help him back into his memory.

After a moment, he remembered vaguely that the person she was referring to was in fact him.

He sighed, all dramatics.

"Fine, you got me there," he said. "Ask your favor."

Price had known Blake since the two were kids and, between them, they pretty much knew the whole of Seven Roads, Georgia. From Becker Farm to the old popular smoking spot for seniors behind the steel mill, they had both done time in the small town and knew it in and out. Even Blake leaving for a decade or so and then marrying a transplant hadn't thrown off her ability to adapt once again to the town's people and ways.

That went double for her managing the contract work she had been doing for several law enforcement agencies around the state while keeping an eye on the local sheriff's department. She had been a one-woman army before coming back. Now, she had her own troops and was unstoppable when she wanted to be.

However, unlike Blake's life trajectory taking her away from Seven Roads before ultimately coming back to town, Price hadn't left McCoy County for more than a week in total since he'd been born at its hospital.

Nineteen years after that, his daughter had been born in the same hospital. Since then, all thoughts of crossing the county line had come to a halt.

There was some rustling on the other end of the line. Blake must have been moving around. She didn't try to lower her words though.

"Can you go look in Josiah Teller's backyard?"

Price pulled the phone away from his ear and eyed it for a second. He put it back against his ear.

"Say again?"

Blake didn't undercut her request with any more sighs. Now she meant business. He straightened on reflex as her tone shifted completely away from friend to a former sheriff on a mission. Favor or not, the change was no joke.

"Josiah said something dug a hole in his backyard but he's sure it was a human who did it, not an animal," she said. "He called the nonemergency line at the department but, given the case I dealt with back in Alabama with burying things, I have all cases involving any kind of potential burial flagged for me and Liam. He has a press issue to deal with and I have the kids out with me now or else I'd go out there myself."

Blake had built one heck of a résumé before returning to Seven Roads, not to speak to what she'd done since she had been back. Price had followed her career like he had been reading a comic book. He knew about the case that had left an impression with her when it came to burials too.

So he didn't voice his concern that it was Josiah Teller who was the one who had called it in.

"You want me to go make sure it isn't anything fishy," he summarized instead.

"Yeah," Blake replied. "I'd send someone else out there who's on duty, but everyone is tied up. Plus, I trust your judgment."

Price knew he was a likable guy. He was confident enough in himself to claim a good personality. But to have Blake trust in him meant a lot more than simply being liked. His chest swelled with pride at it.

He nodded to the phone.

"I'll head that way in ten. I'll call if it's anything worth mentioning."

Blake said thank-you and didn't keep him on the line past that.

Price went straight to the shower, grabbed some pain meds for his headache when he got out and was at Josiah's front door ten minutes after that. There were pros to living in a town as small as Seven Roads. The commute time was almost always snapping-your-fingers quick.

Price knocked on the front door of the two-story, pulling on a professional smile despite nothing on him being professional at the moment. He was dressed in his jeans, tennis shoes and the worn baseball pin-striped button-up he'd had since he was twenty. He had a hat on to cover his still-wet hair but contemplated taking it off. Just because he was off duty didn't mean he should be too slouched since he was doing a favor for the sheriff.

When no one answered after a minute or so, Price's impatience won over his concern. Instead of leaving, he went around to the backyard. The privacy fence was high, but the side yard gate was open.

"Josiah?"

All the houses in the two-road neighborhood were situated on decent-sized lots. Josiah's was no exception. His yard stretched long and wide. There were no trees, but a hammock was set up between two in-ground posts near the patio.

There was no Josiah.

There was a hole.

Price walked over to the disturbed dirt and looked inside of it.

"That's a hole for sure," he commented aloud.

Price tilted his head to the side.

At first, he had pictured something large enough that a person could be put in, simply for the fact that he'd seen one too many horror movies. Then, he had pictured something half that size. Maybe a hole a dog would dig to hide a bone or a toy. He had only imagined one other potential size and it had been a misshapen thing made by a rooting armadillo or roaming raccoon. Maybe an overzealous squirrel.

But what he was looking at didn't match up with any option he had pictured.

Instead, it just looked like something a small child had done while playing. It was a small hole that a shoebox could fit into and that he guessed was made with a gardening tool instead of someone's bare hands.

Price looked around the yard again.

There were no other holes or disturbed spots around.

"Okay, I'm *slightly* intrigued," Price said aloud. He hooked one thumb through his belt loop to rest his hand and used the other to pull out his phone. He took a picture with it and was about to call the sheriff's department to look for Josiah's number when movement flicked out of the corner of his eye.

A few yards away was the back door with a bank of windows on either side. Those windows were covered by curtains and blinds from the inside. The back door, however, seemed to be open.

"Josiah?" Price called out, walking towards it.

He knew Josiah the same way he knew most of Seven Roads. Everyone in town had a story attached to them that the rest of the residents knew. Josiah was a young guy, smart too, but absolutely strange. He quieted when he should talk and when he should be quiet, he gave a sermon. That had become most apparent when he had gone on a tangent about the difference between air vents and air ducts during Mr. McCall Senior's memorial service. While everyone else was doing the small nods and smaller talk, Josiah had been talking commercial use versus residential grade air-conditioning terms. Not the worst thing a person could do, but it had definitely been a story that had stuck.

Maybe that was why Price didn't think too much about the back door being ajar. Or Josiah not answering his call right away. Price was thinking of the man who had taught him about ductwork and not someone who might have been trouble lurking in his house.

It was an oversight on his part.

One that Price realized quickly.

He pushed the door open. It led up through the middle of the house and alongside the stairs.

"Hey Josiah, it's Price Collins. I was told to come out and—"

The movement that had caught his eye flashed again. This time, it was in the form of someone stepping into the hallway, opposite him.

Price knew he was standing on someone else's property. He knew he hadn't been given permission to come inside, just as he was acutely aware that he had no uniform on, no badge to flash and no service weapons or equipment to defend himself.

What he didn't know was what a person dressed all in black, with a ski mask to boot, was doing in Josiah Teller's house.

But he did know he was about to found out.

THERE ARE A lot of situations where a woman might want to meet an attractive man. Out for a night on the town where you and your girls are feeling pretty and flirty? Yes. Walking through the grocery store on a perfect hair day? Absolutely. Just really wanting to get lost in a daydream while you're sitting at a coffee shop, staring idly through the plate-glass windows? Definitely a situation where running randomly into a good-looking man might be a nice occasion.

However, being caught breaking and entering into a house, dressed like a robber, isn't exactly ideal.

JJ mentally swept her own outfit as she looked the man opposite her up and down.

Her hair was braided tight and tucked tighter beneath her mask; the man's hair was curling out from under the edge of a baseball cap. Her black sweater and joggers were baggy enough to hide her curves; the black undershirt clung in an appealing way against an upper body that she assumed was as fit as his arms. Her stance was perfect for being lithe and fleeing the situation, body tilted slightly toward the living room she was closest to; his stance was like his body—he had walled off the exit behind him and seemed ready to close in on her. JJ knew he couldn't see her dark eyes, slightly panicked; she could see the way his bright gaze wasn't moving an inch from her.

The man was handsome. The man was trouble.

JJ moved fast. One second, she was in the hallway, the next she was in the living room and hightailing it to the front door. Adrenaline filled her veins. Panic filled her feet. Her mind went to opening the door; her feet went the other way.

Pain exploded against her hip as JJ hit the hardwood, mere steps away from the entryway. The man wasn't far behind.

No one has perfect balance. You hit the ground, you use the ground to hit whoever you're going up against.

JJ's godfather's words were old but the directive in them was urgent. Instead of scrambling to her feet and trying to recover, she paused. If her pursuer realized she had stalled, it didn't stop him. He was barking something out as he closed the space between them and reaching for her with clear intention of trapping her in that good-looking gaze.

Too bad JJ wasn't going to let that happen.

The second he was close enough she grabbed his wrist.

Then she pulled him.

The man made a startled noise. It was the only thing he could control. JJ escaped being pinned by his falling body by barely a breath of space. His side connected with the ground and JJ used a childhood filled with gymnastic training to spring to her feet.

It was a spot reversal that clearly gobsmacked the man.

JJ was able to double back and run until she was near the back door before he was on her again. This time, it wasn't her bad luck that allowed an opening. It was the man's apparent passion for baseball. He slid like he was going to home in front of a crowded stadium. And he wasn't concerned about taking the ump with him.

They both hit the ground again. This time, JJ went down without a hope of saving herself. Her adrenaline masked the initial pain, but she knew it hurt. The man's weight didn't help matters. She felt his elbow in her back, his knee against her ankle. The rest of him distributed between the two spots.

All of it was an issue.

One that JJ wasn't going to put up with.

She didn't hear her godfather's words of wisdom or any of her trainers barking instructions in her ear. She didn't think of any manual or video she had studied. She simply moved.

With everything JJ had, she became a whirlwind of movement. She threw her head back until it connected with him. Then the rest of her body followed. Her elbow became a hook; her foot became a pendulum. She wasn't sure what worked but knew she had done something when the weight against her disappeared.

When she heard the cussing, she knew it was now or never.

JJ used the narrow hallway to her advantage. The wall to her left became a springboard to help her pinball herself up and out of the house. Not even the wayward punch the man threw against her side slowed her down.

The second her feet touched the back porch, she was running with everything she had. The man, however, didn't know JJ. He didn't know that, while her fighting skills were good, her ability to escape was better. His yells filled the backyard as he followed her.

But as soon as she cleared the back fence, she knew he didn't stand a chance.

Poor man. It must have taken him a bit longer to realize that too.

JJ could still hear him yelling as she made her way into the woods.

Chapter Two

Josiah Teller's backyard became a lot more interesting as the morning turned into afternoon. He had told them until he was blue in the face that nothing in his house was missing or had been disturbed but that hole in the dirt and grass.

That was the thing that he swore had changed.

Price rubbed his jaw and stared down into the small, unassuming thing and felt more grumble in his chest than the storm in the distance could dare create.

Deputy Rose Little, who had only stopped giving him guff about being hit in said jaw before losing it completely half an hour before, stood at his side with such an uninterested expression it almost made Price laugh.

Almost.

His jaw wasn't the only thing sore about what had happened earlier.

"I'm saying it's unrelated," Rose finally decided. "It makes no sense for someone to get that done up and tussle with the law *and* dig a hole. Plus, Josiah said there should be nothing buried here. He bought the house from Ken and Clarice Weathers. You remember them?"

Price nodded. He did.

Rose went on.

"Ken hated dogs and Clarice hated being outside. Together

they wouldn't have had a dog, and a dog is about the only thing I can think would be the reason anything is buried out here." Rose toed at the raised dirt nearest her. "Josiah is always itching for some excitement. I think he made a mountain out of a molehill, and you just got unlucky enough to take the hits when something worth talking about happened."

She patted Price on the shoulder and turned toward the house.

"I'm going to focus on finding that unlucky thing first," she added. "Why don't you use the time to go get some coffee. Looks like you need it. I'll keep you in the loop."

Price hadn't said much since his initial call to the department, the sheriff and Josiah Teller, who had been called away by work and had hightailed it to the local electronics store while Price had been en route to the house Josiah had left behind.

Josiah had profusely apologized, thinking no one was coming anytime soon to discuss the hole.

That apologizing had only tripled when he realized Price had caught someone breaking and entering.

Now, Price felt all talked out.

Though, he guessed, that was mostly from the frustration. Whoever had been in that house had outdone him.

He grumbled.

It wouldn't happen again.

"Just go," Rose said after that grumble cleared. She lowered her voice. "You best believe that news of your fight is already making the Seven Roads laps. I suggest you go take that cup of coffee sooner rather than later."

This time, Price let his frustration melt into defeat.

He knew what Rose was saying without her actually saying it.

He needed to go talk to Winnie before the talk got to her.

Sometimes dealing with a masked intruder was less daunting than dealing with a teenage girl.

Downtown Seven Roads was never a busy place. That stayed mostly true for the weekends. There were the regular walkers who made their way in a pattern across the sidewalks and stores, chatting as they went, and then there were the people who worked at the storefronts who walked between the shops. The Twenty-Two Coffee Shop, however, had become its own localized sensation over the last year or so. Mainly because it was the only coffee shop in town, but also for the popularity of the twins who ran it.

Corrie Daniels, the more popular of the two, was behind the counter and all eyes were on him the second he cleared the door. She was smirking before a word even came out of her mouth.

"I was wondering when you would roll in here." She placed the magazine she was reading down on the countertop and, with obvious attention, eyed his jaw. "I wasn't going to say anything if you looked too beat-up, but you seem good enough now to tease a little." She touched a spot on her jaw and then pointed to him. "Let me know if you need some of my makeup to cover that soon-to-be pretty bruise you've got there."

Price had been friends with Corrie since elementary school, though the title of *friends* was used loosely. The two of them had always just been there, around each other growing up in the same small town they had been born in. *Comrades in arms* is what he once described their relationship. Two people who had once dreamed of crossing the county line and never coming back.

Only to still be in town, annoying each other.

Price paused at the counter and didn't reply directly to

the comment. Instead, he nodded to the hallway that led back to the main office and break room.

"Is she back there?"

Corrie nodded, her smirk turning back into a look of slight boredom.

"Her break just started, but her phone was blowing up before she even stepped foot away from here. Whoever was around you or Josiah's place sure was talking fast. She got the news before me."

Price sighed.

"And what news was that exactly?" He wanted to hear the gossip version so he could have a defense ready to go.

"Oh, you know how it is with Josiah Teller," she started. "He ticked someone off because he was crying wolf about something again and you wanted to save Little Rose the trouble of going out there. But you got cocky and went out without your badge or gun and got your tush handed to you. Then the mass of muscle ran off before you could even stand straight."

Price stared for a moment.

"That's not what happened," he deadpanned.

Corrie shrugged.

"That's the cinematic version going around," she said. "Which means that it was probably Josiah's neighbor—you know, Tacky Tara—who was the one who started it. Remember her retelling of The Great Divorce of the Youngs when we were in high school? She had the whole town thinking that Mr. Young was some kind of mob boss and Mrs. Young had gone through heaven and *h-e*-double-hockey-sticks to escape his grasp."

Corrie clutched at her chest, all dramatics. Then she rolled her eyes.

"When really Mrs. Young was caught with the literal

mailman and all Mr. Young did was pop him once in the eye and then move."

Price remembered the incident, just as he remembered the then-teenage girl Tara who had told anyone who would listen her side of someone else's story.

"In this regard, and this regard only, do I appreciate your brand of nosy," Price had to tell Corrie now. "You at least get the facts straight before you open your mouth."

Corrie smiled sweetly.

"Thank you. I'm glad to be appreciated." She motioned to the hallway. "Now, go set her straight before Tacky Tara's story evolves enough to win an Emmy."

Price nodded.

"Roger that."

The break room was the smallest room in Twenty-Two Coffee Shop but, according to its youngest staff member, that's what made it the coziest. Easy to clean, easy to see and easy to relax in. No matter how stressful the customers became.

Though, *relaxed* isn't the word Price would use to describe what the teenager sitting on the edge of its sofa looked like when he knocked on its open door.

Winnie Collins looked every inch like her mama, but for every single one of those inches, she was Price in personality. Dark eyes narrowed in on him while her mouth thinned into an expression that wasn't a frown, but it wasn't a smile either. It was an in-between look of worry and annoyance.

She stood to her impressive height and closed the distance between them with her index finger outstretched. She didn't poke the skin, but he felt her fingertip hover near his growing bruise.

"Is this the worst of the hits or just the only thing I can see right now?" she asked, instead of giving a greeting.

Price waved her off.

"This was a lucky hit," he said. "I can't even feel it."

Winnie tipped her head to the side and narrowed those eyes again.

"I thought you weren't supposed to be working today. Why were you at Josiah's?"

Price had a rule. He had had it since he brought Winnie home from the hospital and he had kept it during the seventeen years since.

We don't lie to Winnie.

"Your favorite Sheriff Trouble asked me to check out some weird hole dug in Josiah's backyard. I ran into someone who had broken into his house instead. We fought a little, they ran a lot. Lost them out in the woods before Rose showed up." Price smiled. "See? Not as bad as the rumor mill, huh?"

Winnie's eyebrows knitted together. She wasn't upset anymore, but she was confused.

"A hole?"

"That's what I was focusing on too," Price said. "Either way, it's on Little Rose now. I'm only here for some kid, coffee and contemplation."

Winnie didn't look like she wanted to drop the current topic. She opened her mouth to say something, but footsteps made her pause. Price turned to an already-smiling Corrie. He knew what she was going to say before she could even say a word.

She wanted a favor from him.

A gut feeling that proved true with impressive speed.

"Hey, Price, you drove here in your truck, right? Do me a favor and help JJ out?"

Price raised an eyebrow at that.

"JJ?"

"The newest hire," Winnie added from behind him. "Though she isn't new anymore."

Price knew there was a new woman who had been hired part-time, but he only came into the café when Winnie was working. That apparently hadn't synced up with this JJ's schedule yet.

"She's supposed to come in to help me with something in the back, but just called and said she's having car trouble," Corrie said. "She said she could figure something out, but she sounded stressed. Do you think you could swing by and see if you can help her out? Bless her heart, she's a hard worker but I think sometimes she's a little oblivious to things."

Price wanted to point out that the last favor he'd done that day hadn't exactly gone his way, but Winnie thumped his elbow before he could say it.

"Since he's in such a giving mood today, he'll definitely go by and help," she answered for him. "Won't you, Dad?"

Price was still nursing a slight hangover and, despite what he said, his jaw was hurting a little. He also needed to mow the lawn, fix the slow drip in the upstairs bathroom and take a look at the rental property he'd begrudgingly inherited before any more rain came in.

But one thing he had been struggling with since he'd held that little baby in his arms for the first time was another unwritten rule he had become trapped by.

We don't say no to Winnie.

He let out a breath that was mild annoyance and fixed Corrie with an even stare.

"Fine," he said. "But make sure she knows I'm coming. I don't want a Josiah Teller round two surprise today."

Corrie was already pulling out her phone.

"I don't think you have to worry about JJ," she said. "I'm pretty sure that girl is as innocent as they come."

JJ SHOT OUT of the house like the devil was nipping at her heels. She popped the hood of her little Honda and paused as she looked down into the engine bay.

"What can I mess with that will make you not work but not be suspicious?" she asked it out loud. "But also not cost me an arm and a leg to fix?"

She had never been that great at cars. In fact, as far as vehicles went, she only really had a passion for the old motorbike currently hidden in her garage beneath an old sheet and a layer of dust. But there were a few lessons that her godfather had forced her to learn.

JJ mentally scrolled through the reasons she could remember of why a car normally wouldn't start.

"It can't be the battery," she said to herself. "I can't make the alternator or the ignition switch go bad so quickly. I don't know enough about spark plugs to do anything." Her eyes came to a spark plug wire. "Wouldn't that seem suspicious if I unplugged that? I could break a fuse…"

JJ wanted to yell in frustration. She shouldn't have used car trouble as an excuse to not go into the café today. Who would have guessed Corrie would arrange for Winnie's dad to come to the rescue.

"This is ridiculous," she said, exasperated. "No one is as worried about the world as I am. Let's just play it simple."

JJ made the quickest work she could of disconnecting a spark plug wire. Winnie had bragged a few times about her father being capable. He would probably see the problem sooner rather than later then fix it and be on his way. Who was he to be suspicious at all? It wasn't like most people would see JJ and assume she had sabotaged her own car to cover up a lie.

She nodded at her work, shut the hood and hurried back inside.

The pace wasn't a fun one.

She only slowed when she was standing in front of the full-length mirror in her bedroom. Her hair was nice and loose, no longer tight against her head in a braid. Her makeup had been reapplied and she had changed her baggy clothes for a nice, flowy sundress. Her feet were still bare but there was a pair of sandals by the front door that was a far cry from the boots she had been sneaking around in hours beforehand.

As for the bruising, she had gotten lucky.

The man who had fought her had only gotten one good hit in.

One had been enough though.

JJ tenderly touched the spot on her side that she knew for a fact was already bruised.

The light contact made her wince.

That was why she had opted for an excuse to not go into work. It wasn't a normal shift after all. She didn't think she needed much more than a vague car-related issue.

That had been her mistake. JJ had forgotten that she was back in a small town. For better or worse, residents tended to get into everyone's business.

JJ heard a car door shut outside. She gave herself another once-over in the mirror and pulled on a bright, cheery smile.

She would accept Winnie's dad's help, make small talk about the teen and then send him on his way. No muss, no fuss.

Perfect plan.

A knock sounded on the front door.

JJ hid her pain once again and hurried to answer it.

She must have been faster than the man thought she would be. When she opened the door, his head was still turned toward the car in the driveway.

It was the only reason JJ was able to hide the absolute shock that must have gone across her face.

It was clearly the man from Josiah's, even still wearing his baseball shirt.

Had her identity been discovered? Was he there to finish their fight?

But no. His body language was lax, and his attention was clearly on her car.

So, he was Winnie's dad?

But wasn't Winnie's dad a sheriff's deputy?

A cold feeling of unease settled in JJ's gut.

Since coming to Seven Roads, she had been careful not to make any mistakes.

Today, she had not only been caught, she'd been caught by the law.

And now that law was standing in front of her, looking just as good as he had before their fight.

Today really wasn't JJ's day after all.

Chapter Three

Price couldn't say with confidence that he was all that great at understanding the subtleties of women. He didn't have much experience in that department, if he was being honest. Sure, he'd gone on a few dates in the last several years but none of them had exactly panned out.

For one, he wasn't good at being quiet. He was a talker. Had been since he was a kid, would be until he was old and gray. He could probably trace the reason why he loved to chat back to his mother, queen of the talkers. Rest her soul—she wasn't gone but she was constantly driving her second husband up the wall in their home in Las Vegas—she filled every space in a conversation to the brim.

"It's amazing what you end up hearing when you talk too much," she'd always say. "Shows you who people really are when they realize they can't keep you quiet too."

Price had thought the sentiment was ridiculous. Still, he'd managed to pick up the trait.

He listened, sure, but talking was his bread and butter.

That hadn't always been appreciated. Especially on his dates. Though, that also could have had less to do with him dominating the conversation and more that he was dating in Seven Roads. The same place he'd been born. The same place his dates had also been born.

It was hard to connect with someone who knew every little thing about you. From knowing about the unfortunate peeing incident in kindergarten to Jimmy Johnson pantsing you in eighth grade to your grades, fashion choices and tripping during high school graduation. Then there was the fact of holding the single father title at the age of nineteen.

Price was never, not even for one second, ashamed of being a dad. He had never said one bad word about Winnie's mother, and he had never regretted his choices about either one. But he had another rule: if someone spoke about either with any negativity, they were out.

That was why, now in his thirties, he was still single.

It was also why he wasn't as confident as he normally would have been, standing across from JJ Shaw.

First, he didn't know her. A rare occurrence in town.

Second, she did that thing that he believed women had a special power over.

She smiled.

A smile that slowed his mental gears for a moment.

It looked nice but…there was something else there.

Though, maybe that was just Price still off his game from his earlier fight. Or the fact that some strange man was standing at her door.

Price hoped the smile he tugged on was a reassuring one. He took a small step back and jerked his thumb over his shoulder to the car.

"Hey, I'm Winnie's dad," he said in greeting. "I've been sent to help with some car trouble?"

JJ surprised him with a little laugh.

"I was actually about to start googling things. So I'd be lying if I said I wasn't excited at the help." She held out her hand. "I'm JJ. Sorry for the trouble."

Price accepted her hand and shook. There were a few

callouses on her palm. It was an odd contrast to the cheery dress that made his own outfit look dark.

"I'm Price, and it's no trouble," he responded. "There'd really be trouble if I didn't come. Winnie talks highly about you."

JJ stepped back into the house a little to slip on some sandals. They were strappy and made her taller. He had to adjust his gaze a little to meet her eyes again. She averted that gaze quickly as she spoke.

"Oh, that's sweet of her. We haven't had many shifts together yet, but I have to say she's a fun one when we do sync up. And I've definitely heard good things about you. From Corrie too."

She pulled her keys off a hook on the wall and stepped outside. Price made room for her and then some as she walked over to the car in the drive.

"I'm afraid to know what Corrie has to say about me," he admitted. "One time, I accidentally stepped on the back of her shoe and the next day she had the whole school calling me Big Foot. That name stuck for years."

She laughed again but kept her gaze ahead.

"Well, she hasn't been calling you any names around me," she said. "All I hear are stories about your work. You're a sheriff's deputy, right? That must be exciting work."

It hadn't been for years, not until the current sheriff had stumbled upon a homicide after Blake had returned to town. Since then, there had been a shift in the workforce, as with the residents of Seven Roads. It was like they had all been given a wake-up call that said while their town was sleepy, that didn't mean it couldn't also be dangerous.

Price had gotten involved in the last bit of danger, and so had Winnie. It was another reason his earlier scare upset him so much—it worried Winnie. Most likely more than she had admitted.

"It has its moments," he replied.

Where others might have asked more, JJ changed topics to the mission at hand. She gave Price the keys and let him roam around to try and figure out why it wouldn't start.

A few minutes later, he was thankful that he knew enough about cars to notice a spark plug cable had come loose. He put it back, happy with himself, and asked her to try and start the engine.

She obliged but was slow getting into the driver's seat.

When she noticed his attention, she looked a little embarrassed.

"I'm in the middle of renovating a house and it weirdly always makes me sore," she explained.

"You're renovating a house?" He hadn't heard that news.

She paused, a slight wince crossing her face, and nodded.

"It's why I came to town."

Where he expected some more, JJ gave him less.

She settled into the driver's seat and started the car. Which succeeded.

Price gave a thumbs-up.

"Looks like that was our issue," he said when she was back out of the car.

JJ was back to the original smile she'd worn when answering the door.

It was polite.

But it felt off, still.

"Thank you so much for helping," she said. "You saved me a lot of trouble and I'm sure Corrie will appreciate it. I'm actually already late helping her."

Her gaze, once again, cut away from him.

Was she shy?

Did he make her nervous?

No matter the answer, Price realized it wasn't his business. Whether he was making her uncomfortable or not, he needed to leave. Instead of forcing them both to make small talk, he decided to give them an out.

"I'm just glad it was something I could help with." He clapped his hands together and took a step back. "If that's all, I'll leave you to it. I have some work to wrap up at the department."

This time, dark eyes swung to his with a quickness that nearly froze him to the spot.

"I didn't realize you were still working right now."

He laughed and pointed to his jaw. JJ might not have been keen to look him in the eye, but he had already seen her sneak a peek at the bruise.

"I have a bone to pick with someone and the sooner I pick it, the better this town will sleep."

JJ's eyes widened. He waved off what must have been concern.

"Don't worry. I know I don't look the most professional but believe you me, I don't suffer an offense long."

He nodded to her, said he hoped she had a good rest of the day and did another little nod when she thanked him again. It was true he was going to look for the meaning behind Josiah's break-in, just as he was going to find the intruder, but for now he was going to go home.

Seven Roads might have been more interesting in the last year or so but that didn't mean it was a hustling, bustling place. He could take his time with this one. Or, at least, take a few hours.

So he fixed JJ Shaw in his rearview mirror and pointed his truck in the direction of Crawley Court, ready to make the five-minute drive home full of music and a few low cusses as he remembered someone had landed a good hit on him.

But no sooner was he out of the neighborhood that he got a call.

It was Rose's number.

Price answered with an annoyed threat.

"If you're calling to rub it in again or make some joke about me being a punching bag, I'm going to hang up."

Rose wasn't.

Her voice was hard. Her words were fast.

"Something happened to Josiah Teller. There's a ton of blood in his house and he's nowhere around."

"What? What do you mean there's blood?"

Price was already mentally switching routes.

There was movement on Rose's side of the call. Someone was talking in the background, but she answered him first.

"I came back to take better pictures of that damn hole of yours and instead found the front door smashed open and enough blood through the bottom floor to tell me someone was fighting for their life." She must have moved the phone. Static pulsed between them for a moment. Then her voice was nothing but cold. "Darius is already out looking for him, but I can't believe, if this was Josiah, that he'll last long wherever he is."

Price gripped the steering wheel. His knuckles went white.

"I'm on my way."

JJ SWITCHED HER high-heeled sandals for flats the second Price Collins was gone.

Deputy Collins.

"How bad is my luck?" she asked the house, grabbing her purse and then locking up behind her.

As far as she could tell, Price, at the very least, hadn't

seemed too suspicious of her. Not of her car troubles, the pain she had been unable to hide or her appearance. She wasn't sure how aware of her height, or eyes for that matter, he had been during their run-in earlier that day, but was glad he had gone when he did.

She didn't like being caught off guard, and she had been twice that day.

And by the same man too.

It was unsettling.

JJ tried to push the feeling off as she started her drive to the café. Like she often did on her way into and out of work, she let her mind wander down a familiar path. The list of five addresses she had memorized before coming back to Seven Roads.

Josiah's house had been low on the list. JJ had only moved it up when she heard about someone digging in his backyard by chance that morning while picking up some milk from the grocery store. Josiah had been wondering to the cashier if he should call the sheriff's department. Apparently, he had.

Their speed and attention had definitely surprised JJ. She should have waited to do her own search until they had come and gone.

But…if anyone *had* been snooping around Josiah's home… Did that mean that it really could be him?

That possibility had lit a fire under her backside. So much so that she had been careless. Price sneaking up on her had been the first and—she vowed—last time she let her guard down.

JJ rolled her window down, put her hand out the window a little and sighed into the humidity that came in. Despite her clumsiness, she believed she'd executed a thorough search. Josiah didn't have a safe, so his official documents had been easy enough to find. Nothing was out of the ordinary or suspicious. Even his personal laptop had been boring, aside from a heavy indication that he was a more than avid gamer. He had a family photo album next to his coffee table and those pictures were of people that JJ didn't recognize at all. Though, she had taken her own picture of some of the faces, just in case.

The only thing she hadn't had a chance to check had been the backyard.

If Josiah had been hiding something, would he have buried it?

And, if he had, then who had dug it up?

Why had Josiah reported it if so?

JJ didn't often drink, but she sure felt the urge as her frustration rose. At the same time, however, she was thankful for it. If she was having this much trouble finding her brother, then hopefully that meant they were too.

She took that thought to heart again and focused on her drive. It wasn't until she was passing the Lawrence Neighborhood entrance sign that she realized she had taken the long way to the café. It was the road that led between Lawrence and Becker Farm. A nice little drive with scenery that opened up to fields and trees on either side. Good for a cluttered mind.

JJ decided that today must have been a coincidence. That Josiah Teller wasn't special, just someone who had made a big deal out of nothing. She would go to the next person on the list in a few days, after her run-in with Price settled down.

Her gaze wandered from the trees at her right to the field on her left. There were no other cars on the road ahead or behind her, so it was a leisurely thing to do.

It was a miracle she saw him at all.

Movement in the field pulled her attention. At first, JJ wasn't sure what she was seeing. She lifted her foot off the gas pedal and squinted at the thing stumbling toward the road.

When she realized it was a person, stumbling through the tall grass, she put on her hazards and pulled off onto the shoulder.

It wasn't just a person. It was someone who was obviously struggling.

They moved a few steps, fell a little, caught themselves and then kept coming.

It wasn't until she was out of the car, cell phone in hand, that they saw her too.

The man stopped.

He said something but she couldn't hear him.

Then he dropped.

JJ's reflexes had her across the road, over the wire fence and streaking across the distance between them with efficient speed. She was barely out of breath when she made it to the man's side.

She had 9-1-1 up and ringing the moment she saw he was struggling.

He was covered in blood. From head to toe.

His eyes were closed. He didn't move as JJ asked after him.

It was only after the dispatcher answered that JJ made another startling discovery.

It wasn't just a man.

It was Josiah Teller.

Chapter Four

Lane Medical wasn't that bad for a county place. It had serviced locals from Seven Roads nicely through the years and, since it was located closer to the town than the neighboring city, at any one time it housed people who Price knew. Staff, patients, visitors. He hadn't ever visited the hospital without running into someone.

After coming in hot with Rose, he tried to avoid all of the above as he made his way up to the second floor while the deputy was snarled in the emergency room, waiting to talk to the attending doctor.

The surgery ward was an entirely different beast than the general population rooms downstairs. Everything was shining, bright and smelled like disinfectant. Even the resident behind the front desk at the mouth of the main hallway had a neater look to her that those battling in the ER below didn't have the luxury to maintain.

This face was familiar and unavoidable.

Thankfully, that wasn't exactly a bad thing.

"Deputy Price!"

Lily Ernest was one of those people that slightly skewed Price's perception of time. She was the legendary medical examiner Doc Ernest's eldest daughter, but Price still remembered her as a baby, as a kid and then as a teenager who was only a few years older than Winnie. Now? It bowled him over how adult she looked in scrubs. The image clashed with the memories of her toddling around her mother.

It made Price think of Winnie. He still paused on occasion by the growth chart he'd notched into the doorframe of her bedroom at home.

But, just as quickly as he thought of his daughter and how kids never kept, Price reminded himself that he wasn't there for a social visit. He buttoned up his parental awe and gave Lily a polite but curt nod.

"Hey there, Lily. You doing okay?"

Lily tapped her name tag.

"It's nice to be on rotation here, I won't lie. Mom's a bit disappointed I'm not in with her though." She pointed down, meaning the morgue in the hospital's basement. "One day she'll realize I really have no plan to work below sea level."

Her little laugh was kind.

It was also gone quickly. Her gaze dropped to where his badge would usually be, and she added a thought in a much lower voice.

"If you're here to talk to a surgeon, our very best is currently in an emergency surgery. I'm not sure I can help with anything else."

Lily knew she couldn't openly talk about a patient, especially to the law without consent. That probably went double for someone not even in uniform. So, she'd given him what he wanted to know without saying it directly.

She was definitely her mother's daughter.

"If I wanted to wait for the surgery to end, could I do that in the lobby?" Price jerked his thumb over his shoulder and down the hall to the surgery suite's lobby. He'd only had to wait there twice in his Seven Roads life. If the Good Samaritan was still around, they would be there.

Lily nodded and confirmed his hope.

"Yes. There's only one other person in there at the moment so it won't be crowded."

Price gave the girl a genuine smile.

"I'll go do that then. Thanks."

Price followed the hallway through two turns and stepped into the surgery suit's lobby with a growing fire in him. He was angry that Josiah had gone from being fine that morning to needing emergency surgery that afternoon. It also pricked at Price's guilt. Had he caught the masked man earlier, would this have happened?

It was a what if that he was trying to push aside to focus on getting as much information from the Good Samaritan as possible. They needed to catch who did this to Josiah now.

Not later.

Unlike the emergency room lobby, this one was small and closed in with only one door for guests, one door for staff that led in the opposite direction and one door to the bathroom. The two rows of uncomfortable-looking chairs were empty but that last door opened right as Price stepped inside.

He had already teed up several questions for the Good Samaritan, ready to be fast and to the point. However, he stopped short when the person in question caught his eye.

"JJ?"

JJ Shaw was still wearing her summer dress but, this time, it was stained crimson. Still, she managed another smile that took in Price's attention and whirled it around all at once.

FLY UNDER THE RADAR, my butt.

"Deputy Collins," JJ said in greeting.

She didn't know what else to say past that. The moment she found Josiah she had known she would be talking to McCoy County law enforcement and, yet, she hadn't thought it would be him.

Wasn't he off duty?

"Twice in one day," he said. "We should get a bingo card going."

Three times, she thought, but who was counting?

Price's gaze dropped to her body. JJ resisted the urge to cover up. He hadn't been the only person to stare at the blood on her dress since she'd arrived. If the cotton was on the other foot, she would have done the same.

"It's not mine," she assured him. JJ waved her hand over the parts of her dress most stained. "A few of the emergency staff tried to wrangle me into a room but, like I told them, this belongs to that poor man." She paused. "I'm assuming that's why you're here? I'm the one who found the man in the field."

Price's gaze was still on her dress. He nodded absently then held up a finger.

"Hey, I need to ask you some questions, but could you give me one second?"

JJ blinked.

"Um, of course. Yeah."

He spun on his heel and was out of the room in a flash. If he wasn't such an easy man to read, she would have been worried that he'd put two and two together. That standing there in her flats, she was the same height and relative size as the person he had fought with that morning. That common sense would make her the top suspect in what had happened to Josiah.

But JJ wasn't getting the impression that Deputy Collins was ready to bust her.

Still, she decided to keep standing just in case. If he did come back in, cuffs out and accusations flying, she wasn't just going to stay put.

The houses left on her list could be searched without a backstory or a pleasant smile and a part-time job at a café. Sure, if her cover was blown then it would make things harder. Not impossible, just more complicated.

JJ didn't need to be JJ Shaw to find her brother.

She was plenty enough, name or no name.

The thought stayed her nerves. She loosened the new tension in her shoulders but made sure not to seem too relaxed. She marveled at the fact that, once again, she had gone from a plan of staying under the radar in Seven Roads to meeting the law three times in one day.

The *same* man too.

Deputy Collins was back in the lobby in less than five minutes. He came in apologizing for the delay and holding a plastic bag, not cuffs, in his hand.

"Don't let this make you think you're going to be here all day or anything, but I thought, no matter how long, you probably don't want to just be sitting in that."

It took JJ a second to realize what he meant.

He passed the bag over. She peeked inside.

It was a set of scrubs.

His gaze went to her dress again. He pointed to the bag.

"A friend of mine works here and she seems about your size," he added. "I figured wearing this would be more comfortable."

JJ hadn't expected that.

"Oh, I couldn't accept this," she tried. "I'm okay, really."

Price waved his hand, and the thought, off.

"Think of it this way. This is just as much for the rest of us as it is for you," he said. "I'm not sure I can hold a conversation without staring. I'm thinking that the rest of the hospital probably isn't going to let you leave without doing the same."

He was right, of course.

Her walking around covered in blood wasn't helping the whole beneath-the-radar thing either.

JJ smiled.

"I guess you're right. I'll—I'll change then. Thank you."

There he went, waving her off again.

"Here in Seven Roads, we watch out for each other. It's no big deal." He dropped into a seat near the door. "Take your time. I'll be here."

She bowed a little, went to the bathroom and found herself slowing as she did just that. There really was a lot of blood, the more she looked at her reflection. There had been no way to get Josiah to her car and avoid it. It was a fact she had come to terms with quickly once Josiah had stopped moving. When he went limp, that had been when she had decided to completely commit to not caring about avoiding the mess. JJ had pulled him through the field, put him in her car and driven with speed to the hospital.

The attending doctor had told her the time she had saved instead of waiting for an ambulance had probably saved his life.

He hadn't known that her reasoning behind the move had nothing to do with the man and everything to do with the simple reason that she hadn't wanted her call to be registered at the sheriff's department.

That was a trail she couldn't easily cover up.

JJ looked at her hands. They were stained but clean.

It should have thrown her. It should have made her feel something like sadness or panic or worry.

Instead, she was trying to calculate the possibilities that had led Josiah from his house to that field.

There hadn't been a lot of blood on the ground where she had first found him. Not enough to show that he'd been attacked in the immediate area but then again, she hadn't had time to search either. His house had been a few miles away but surely he couldn't have walked like that in the same condition. Did that mean he'd been attacked in the distance between?

And by who?

Josiah wasn't her brother. He had an adoption record, sure, but he'd been adopted as a toddler, not a baby. That struck him from her list.

So had what happened to him been just bad timing on her part?

Her search put Josiah in the spotlight but someone else had already planned on fighting with him?

There was no way to know until she got more information. JJ removed her dress and started to put on the green scrubs. She made sure not to look in the mirror as her bare back came into view. The scar was small, but the memory tied to it was better left out of sight.

Maybe that's why Josiah hadn't affected her so much.

It wasn't the first time she had seen something like that.

JJ folded her dress, placed it in the bag and straightened her new clothes. The scrubs fit her nicely.

Price had a good eye.

Well, at least for clothes.

He still had no idea she was the masked person from that morning.

She was going to have to work hard to keep that from happening.

She went back into the lobby to tell him thank you but hesitated before she could say a word. Like in Josiah's house that morning, JJ could with absolute sincerity say that Price was a good catch. Attractive, attentive and as far as she knew from talk around town and knowing Winnie, a good dad too. There was also a calm about him. He seemed more collected than she would have thought was normal.

He was a good man, most likely.

Probably a good deputy also.

Too bad for him his luck ran out when he met her.

Chapter Five

The field had been for sale since the late nineties. No one had bought it in the years between then and now. What was more, no one would buy it in the future. It wasn't Old Man Becker's land, but it might as well have been.

"No one wants to be next to Old Man Becker's land, so it's been sitting empty for years," Price told JJ. He pointed toward the trees that lined the field in the distance. "There's an access road there that technically cuts the Becker land off from this but, well, it's usually only used by the workers and teens off doing something their parents don't want them knowing about. You said Josiah was coming from that way, toward the county road?"

JJ had put her hair up in a ponytail. It swished from side to side as she turned to the direction Josiah had come.

"I can't for sure say where he started but he definitely was coming from that direction."

They had already run down everything that JJ had seen and done since Price had left her house. Then she had said it all again to Rose when she had come upstairs to the surgery suite's lobby. JJ had been the one nice enough to offer to take them out to the exact place she had found Josiah before Rose had brought it up herself.

Then Price had been the one to offer her the ride.

"Winnie'll have my head if she knows I'm not being as courteous as ever," he had defended himself to Rose's eyebrow raise. "Plus, it's not like we have a lot of manpower to push off everything on you and Darius. I'll get the story from her, take some pics, mark with a flag and wait for y'all to come out."

Rose must have been more stressed than usual. She dropped the subject with a quick thanks. Then she'd gone to talk to Lily, who had gone wide-eyed at the actual appearance of a uniform and badge.

Now, the field in front of Price and JJ was hot, bare and sporting a trail of blood that led him right to the tree line and back to the access road. There the trail stopped altogether. JJ followed but kept her eyes to the ground. She didn't speak until she was at his side.

"There's not enough blood here," she said after a moment. She ran her finger, pointing down at the ground and back toward where she had originally found Josiah. "There's more back there because he stopped but there's only some spots leading back to here." She nodded to the road. "And since it ends at the road, I'm guessing that means he definitely didn't get his injuries out here. He was either dumped here by car or escaped from one."

Price felt his eyes widen. A half smile tugged up the corner of his lips. JJ saw the change and immediately shook her hands in defense.

"I watch a lot of crime series," she said hurriedly. "There was an episode like this on an old show I watched. The woman escaped her kidnappers, and we spent half of the episode trying to figure out where the original attack took place."

Price nodded.

"Well, however you got there, you're not wrong." He put

his hands on his hips and looked down at the last drop of blood in the area. "It definitely seems like Josiah exited a vehicle here."

But had anyone followed him?

"Why didn't anyone stop him from going through the field?"

Price turned back to JJ again.

Her brow was drawn in.

"I mean, I guess if someone was after him, they could have been hidden in the tree line while I saw to Josiah," she said. "That could have been his good luck out of all of this. I showed up when I did and spooked whoever did that to him."

Price nodded. He hadn't told JJ about how they had found Josiah's house. It was part of an ongoing investigation and, even though he had no quarrels with JJ, he didn't see the need to inform her of it. She had already done more than enough.

"Seven Roads might be small, but our Detective Williams is mighty," he said. "We'll get this figured out in no time."

JJ straightened her back. She nodded but didn't respond past that. Instead, she pulled her cell phone from her pocket and read a text in silence. Price used that time to mark the area. When he was done, JJ looked apologetic.

"If there's nothing else you need me for, could I go home?" She motioned to her clothes. "The scrubs are nice, but I wouldn't mind a quick shower."

Price felt bad he hadn't suggested it first. He walked her back through the field, both minding to step on the path they had carefully made before, and stopped by the hood of her car.

"Just so you know, this isn't exactly the natural speed

of Seven Roads," he said. "It's usually a quiet place. Well, minus the gossip."

He grinned.

JJ opened her car door and let her hand rest on the top of the door.

There was some dried blood near her wrist.

"Don't worry, I've seen worse." Her frown went deep. Then it swirled into a small smile of explanation. "I've lived in a few big cities before coming here. This place is silent compared to those." She patted the top of the door. "Let me know if you need anything else from me. You have my number and know where I live. And, I guess, where I work too."

Price confirmed he did.

Before she could slide into her seat though, he reached out to stop her. Their hands didn't touch but it was enough to make JJ pause. She gave him a questioning look.

"Sorry," he said, pulling back. "But do you think you could do me a favor? Could you not tell Winnie about any of this until I talk to her first? The news will probably still get to her before I can but just in case it's slow today, I'd like to try."

JJ smiled.

"Don't worry. The most I'll do today is text Corrie to reschedule. If she needs more, I'll cite car trouble again. After that, I'm staying myself right on my couch."

JJ BROKE INTO the house in complete silence. No alarm beeps, no indoor chatter, no breaking glass or scraping metal. Nothing came before she slipped into the back door and nothing came after she closed it back up tight behind her.

The Alberts were on vacation and had never been a fan of digital security systems. They were from an older generation and had lived in Seven Roads since the seventies. If it wasn't for their kids probably insisting they lock their doors, they seemed to believe that their neighbors should be trusted no matter what.

That was probably why they barely made an effort to hide their spare key beneath the mat on the back porch.

Good for them, better for JJ.

She made her way across the hardwood until she turned into what looked like a guest bedroom. It was easy to navigate with the light from outside peeking through the small gaps between the curtains.

It was even easier when JJ used a gloved hand to make a bigger gap in the opening.

There were two people still milling around Josiah's house. Crime scene tape was on the front door and from her vantage point, she could see one of the uniformed men was making use of the back door. He wore gloves and, she bet, booties. One of the two also had a camera bag slung across his shoulder as he stood there.

So Josiah's attack had most likely occurred in his house.

The same house she had been searching hours before.

Which was bad for two different reasons.

One, it meant that whoever had done the deed had missed her and Price. Which would explain why Price was so obviously invested in the case, despite being off duty.

He probably felt some kind of misplaced guilt for not being able to protect Josiah.

Because he most likely thought that the masked person he had tussled with that morning was the very same person who had landed Josiah in such a state.

Which brought on the second, not-so-great problem.

The search for the masked person was now the top priority of the department.

JJ rubbed the side of her index finger with her thumb. The glove was smooth at both spots. She knew she didn't leave any evidence behind during her search of Josiah's home…but that sureness had rested on the fact that no one would be doing an in-depth search of the place behind her.

Had she made any mistakes in covering her tracks?

Was there anything in there that could tie her to the crime scene?

"No," she whispered to herself.

Still, she couldn't feel completely at ease about it.

This was the second person on her list who she had crossed off and she'd managed to get into not one but two things of hot water alongside of her goal.

JJ decided then and there she would cool off her search for a bit.

She wanted to find her brother but, more than anything, she *needed* to find him.

And she needed to find him before *they* did.

JJ stayed in the Alberts' home until eventually all law enforcement left. If they found anything tying her to the scene, she never got a call or visit once she returned home. It should have made her rest easier but falling asleep that night was more difficult than she thought it would be.

She thought about Josiah falling in the field.

She thought about the blood on their clothes.

She thought about waiting alone in the lobby as he was rushed past to surgery.

JJ wondered if he was doing better. She wondered if he was alone.

Then, because her life had had moments of intense cruelty woven into its fabric, her thoughts slid even further back in time.

She saw her dark hair hanging down, reaching toward

the roof of the car. There was glass everywhere. There was blood too.

There was no use in JJ squeezing her eyes shut. Then, or now. The image was there, and it would stay there for a while. So she embraced the pain and let her eyes lose focus on the ceiling above her now.

Like she'd told Price earlier, she had seen much, much worse than Josiah Teller in that field.

Chapter Six

Josiah Teller survived his surgery. A week later, he was recovering well in a suite in Lane Medical.

"He remembers someone knocking on his front door, but after that he said he can't recall a thing." Detective Williams had his arms crossed over his chest. Outsiders might think he was being nonchalant, but Price knew him well enough to understand he was brimming with anger.

An entire week had gone by and not one stitch of evidence or a lead had been found about Josiah's attacker.

And now he was having to admit that to their newly returned Sheriff Weaver.

Liam sat at the head of the meeting table, fiddling absently with his wedding band. He tilted his chin to the side a little in thought.

"The doc says it could be a trauma response given how violent the attack seemed to be," he said. "That or the very real possibility that the physical injury was too much. Either way, I don't think we can bank on Josiah remembering anytime soon."

Price's coffee mug between his hands was empty. He'd finished part of a patrol before joining the recap and was starting to feel the lack of caffeine now. He had already been feeling frustration way before Sheriff Weaver had entered the building.

"I've been visiting Josiah and each time we talk, we always find our way back to the fact that Josiah really can't figure out why anyone would attack him or go through his house," Price added.

"It could have been random," Rose offered. She was standing in the doorway of the meeting room, paperwork in her hand. She was on the other side dealing with a public intoxication arrest near the county line. She pointed in the direction of the area of the sheriff's department that housed the two holding cells. "My drunk friend earlier was willing to fight anyone and everyone just because they were there. It could have been kind of the same thing. Our attacker did what they did simply because Josiah opened the door."

"But then what about their stint in the house that morning?" Darius asked. He turned his attention to Price. "The guy you fought came back. Whether that was for an object in Josiah's house or Josiah himself, it doesn't read as random. They came to Josiah for a reason."

That was the sticky part. If one of the two events hadn't happened it would have made more sense, but with the two it was tripping them all up. And it wasn't like they could simply make it all clear. That didn't mean they would stop trying to though. Darius was still the detective of the department, and he was still putting in his best. Price, guilt aside, had returned to his normal daily routines.

At least in body.

In mind, he was still in his fight against the masked man in Josiah's house.

If he had subdued him, then would Josiah have almost died?

Price let go of the *what-ifs* as the meeting concluded. He finished out his shift and found himself driving in the direction of the only coffee shop in town. It was just after four and Winnie had arrived right before him from school.

"Don't tell me you're going for another coffee," Winnie said in greeting from behind the counter. "You're too old to have one this late." She had a textbook open, a highlighter in one hand.

The sight warmed him.

Price had never been the greatest at school. There was something about putting pencil to paper that had never worked well for him. That and he'd spent most of his academic career talking and playing around instead of focusing on the task at hand. Winnie's mother had been different. Her attention had always been on studying. It had been the people part of school she hadn't been a fan of at all.

Winnie?

She was split between the two.

She brought home *A*s, studied religiously and had won two spelling bees in her time. She also was good at the talking bits. People liked being around her. Price had often gotten compliments about how polite she was too. He had been rabble-rousing then, and now his kid was soothing the old annoyances he'd left behind.

It made him proud.

It also made him sure of one thing: Winnie Collins was going places.

And, when she finally went to those places?

He was gone too.

Price reached across the space between them and gave her a light thump on the forehead.

"I'll remind you that you called me old when you're my age," he said. "I bet you won't joke about it then."

Winnie didn't dodge the little hit but brushed it off. She

didn't give up her highlighter though. Instead, she used it to point toward the back.

"I can make you the normal but fair warning, Corrie just got a call and she got that face she normally does when something exciting just happened."

Price glanced in that direction.

"Something exciting?"

Winnie sighed.

"I suspect she'll tell you all about it once she sees you."

Price was already angling his body toward the door.

"You know, you might be right," he said. "I think I should cut down on the caffeine. I'll just come back to grab you after shift. I'll stay in the car though."

Winnie laughed. Price might have liked to talk a lot, but gossip was a double-edged sword he'd been cut by plenty of times since becoming a young father. He didn't like indulging in it unless he had to. Winnie was more or less the same. She'd often rolled her eyes at Corrie's need to tell her everyone else's business.

Not to Corrie's face though. Winnie was, once again, the polite Collins.

She waved bye and Price was back in his truck.

It felt too early to go home, but he wasn't about to go back to the department. Price scanned the parking lot. It took him a few beats to realize he was looking for JJ's car. She must have gotten off work earlier.

He wondered how she was doing. Josiah had said she had visited him once in the hospital since he'd gotten out of surgery, but that had been when Price was on duty.

Word had traveled around that she'd been the one to find Josiah in the field, but Winnie had assured him that while a few more people had come to the coffee shop looking for her, JJ had seemed to stay out of the way of most people's rapid-fire questioning. That was good, he'd decided. She probably needed some peace after everything she'd seen.

Price nodded to his own thoughts and went back to trying to figure out his next destination when the door to the coffee shop swung open. Corrie was indeed excited about something. She was visibly bouncing when Price made eye contact with her through the windshield.

She made a stop motion and was at his truck door all within what seemed like one quick movement.

Corrie wasn't smiling but she wasn't frowning either. Her voice however was sweet with the syrup of a favor.

"Hey there, Price," she said. "This sure is fate catching you here."

Price's eyebrow rose at that.

"You do know my daughter works here, right?" he deadpanned.

She waved that off and dove in.

"I mean, when I need a really big favor, you just so happen to be around. It's kismet!"

During high school, Price wouldn't have called his relationship with Corrie Daniels that much more than an acquaintance that *sometimes* bordered on a casual friendship. Now, in their thirties, he was starting to realize somewhere along the line that had changed. Corrie was now someone who looked after Winnie, teased him about his lack of a dating life, questioned his choices and, apparently, had no hesitation in asking for favors.

Price wasn't sure if he liked this change.

Just as he wasn't sure he'd like a favor that had her this animated.

He narrowed his eyes, suspicious.

"Fate *and* kismet," he repeated. "If you say *destiny* next, I'm out before I hear your ask."

Corrie was unperturbed. Her question didn't come with the fancy buzzword though.

"How do you feel about going to a fun little party tomorrow night as our plus-one?"

That surprised him. He didn't know which point to land on first.

"Party? Our?"

She jerked her thumb back at the coffee shop.

"It's a business bureau thing in the city, mainly meant to network. Originally, it was supposed to be Cassandra going but she can't with the baby. Then I was going to go but, well, something just came up that I need to do instead."

"And so you're asking *me* to go? You know I don't work here, right?"

Corrie rolled her eyes.

"I'm asking *you* to be the plus-one to *JJ*, who's been nice enough to agree to go and schmooze a little on our behalf."

Price was less sarcastic in his response.

"JJ's going?"

She nodded.

"I'd send you with Winnie but it's an adult soiree with drinks and the like. Plus, I figured since your social life could use a boost, it might be good for you to go too. That and I feel bad sending our quiet JJ out to battle alone." Corrie slapped her hands together. "Y'all only have to fake nice and chat for an hour. You'll have my gratitude for life. What do you say?"

Price didn't have to think about it long.

"What's the dress code?"

JJ ENDED HER call with Corrie and left her cell phone on the coffee table. She left her house soon after.

The sun wasn't setting but the heat wasn't as high as

it had been during the day. A fact that made her exercise clothes less stifling. Even the small bag she was wearing across her chest wasn't as uncomfortable as it would have been had they been in the thralls of a southern summer. She adjusted it as she drove to the park near Main Street. She adjusted it again once she was outside and walking the beginning of the path.

Seven Roads wasn't that difficult of a place.

It was small but spread out enough that not everyone who lived within the town limits was on top of each other all of the time. Which meant she could do something as innocuous as jogging to get her close to Jamie Bell's home without raising any suspicion.

JJ started her run slow.

Her leg muscles thanked her for the act of mercy.

Since her fight and run-in with Deputy Collins, her ribs had let her know quickly that any exercise was a no-go for a while. The forced break from working out had also bled into her search. She had taken the last week to be as normal as possible instead. Partly, she was waiting for the potential other shoe to drop from her break-in at Josiah's. Partly, because even without anyone pointing fingers at her, the town's attention had slightly turned her way.

So, she had waited.

Then she'd heard that Jamie Bell was about to leave town on a three-month-long business trip.

Which meant searching his house was now or—three months later.

While JJ was good at playing house by herself for a week, three months was too long. That didn't mean she was going to make the same mistake as she did going into Josiah's home. This time, she was going to scout the place longer, only going in when she was sure no one else was around.

And if she found proof that he was the one she'd been looking for?

Then you'll what? she thought to herself, not for the first time. *Tell him that you're his biological sister who isn't actually dead and that you're back in town to make sure the people who almost killed you don't try and kill him?*

JJ picked up her pace. She shook her head slightly at how ridiculous it all sounded.

However, that didn't mean it wasn't true.

That's why she had to be careful, even when she needed to be fast.

The park around her was replaced by the neighborhood that shared a sidewalk with it. Trees were sparse, manicured yards were not. There was a homeowners association. The only one in all of Seven Roads.

Jamie Bell was making decent money as a travel writer.

If he ended up being her brother, JJ made a mental note to be proud.

Until then, she passed by his house at a slow clip and took in as many details as she could.

Two-story. Twelve hundred or so square feet. No visible security cameras or a doorbell camera. The garage was single-car and closed. A vehicle was in the driveway, but it didn't match the SUV he usually drove. JJ had heard he had a boyfriend but didn't know what kind of car he used, only that he lived across town and lived with and took care of his grandfather.

They were probably preparing for him to leave the next day.

She kept on jogging until she was well past the house. An old frustration welled up inside of her as the concrete passed beneath her feet with each new step. She was looking for a needle in a stack of needles…while pretending she wasn't.

All while racing against someone else looking for the same needle.

She wished it was easier.

She knew why it couldn't be.

She—

"JJ?"

JJ stopped in her tracks. She'd been so focused on Jamie's house in the distance, she had let her guard down to the street behind her. A truck was idling on the other side of the two-lane road.

The man smiling at her through his open truck windows could not have surprised her more.

"Deputy Collins?"

Price looked like he was about to say something clever but in another unforeseen twist of fate, JJ's plans of staying beneath everyone's radar went up in smoke.

Literally.

A small explosion tore through the small neighborhood around them.

JJ covered herself in reflex.

It was only after Price was out of the truck and yelling at her that she realized whatever had happened was far enough off that she was fine.

But the same couldn't be said for the two-story home five houses away from them.

JJ couldn't believe it, even as she saw the newly erupted flames at its side.

It wasn't just someone's house.

It was Jamie Bell's.

Chapter Seven

Something blew up. Not large enough to destroy the house but enough that flames were already lapping at the wall on one side.

Price had felt the impact in his truck. At JJ's side, he could easily see the chaos.

"Are you okay?" He used one hand to pat her back and arm, even as she nodded. That was all the confirmation he needed. Price pushed his phone in her hand and started to run.

"Call this in and get back," he yelled over his shoulder.

He didn't know if she responded. There was no time to talk about anything.

A car was in the driveway of the affected house.

Someone was probably home.

The heat from the fire met Price as his feet hit the driveway. The front porch wasn't on fire, but it was close enough that Price didn't slow down until he was rounding the side yard and tearing through the back. He tripped in his haste but started yelling out for the homeowners before he was at the back door.

"Sheriff's department," he yelled in reflex. "Is anyone inside?"

Glass was breaking somewhere, probably from the heat, but no other sound came through. Price tried the door. It was locked. He called out again but nothing. He took a few steps back and checked the only window next to him. It was also locked.

He was going to have to break either the door or the window.

Price ran the fastest math he could and decided the window would be the best option. No sooner than he went for the flowerpot he intended to use to break it did someone push past him.

JJ had something in her hands and set to the door without a word.

"What are you doing?" he yelled out. "You need to lea—"

The door opened. JJ cut him off with her own shout.

"Jamie Bell and his boyfriend might be in here!"

Then she turned and ran right into the house.

Price's lack of time, once again, kept him from reacting the way he wanted to. Instead, he followed her.

The layout of the house was nearly the same as Price's. The back half of the house had a small bathroom, a dining room and a kitchen opposite the living room. Stairs ran between the latter two.

The explosion had originated in the kitchen. Heat and smoke radiated into the hallway with intensity. Price placed an arm over his mouth and peered into the destruction.

No bodies as far as he could see.

JJ must have concluded the same. She was already running up the stairs.

Price followed, skipping two steps at a time.

Once they were at the landing, they split up. JJ went to one of the doors on the left and Price went right.

It was a bedroom and, thankfully, there wasn't much to it either. A bed, dresser, and nightstands.

No Jamie Bell or his boyfriend.

Maybe the car Price had run by in the driveway had been left behind and there was no one in the—

A scream came from somewhere else on the second floor.

It was JJ.

Price backtracked faster than he had run into the bedroom and went to the room opposite. It was a lot less simple.

The bedroom was twice as large, had more furniture cluttering the open space, and had, not one, but three people in it.

One was a man on the ground.

One was a man in a hooded jacket.

One was JJ and she had her hands on the jacket of the latter while standing over the former.

"Price," she yelled.

There was no directive in it, but he understood the assignment, even if he didn't have the context. He closed the space between them, just as the man in question threw out a punch to get JJ off him.

It was a hit that didn't land. At least not against JJ.

The man's fist connected with Price's open palm right before Price sent out his own hit. The man staggered as the punch landed against his jaw. The sudden imbalance knocked JJ off the hooded man's jacket.

But she wasn't done.

Price watched as she launched an all-out attack.

An attack that wasn't bad at all.

The second she was in striking distance, she struck.

When the man dodged and returned a hit, she dropped down.

Before Price could intervene, she swept her leg out.

The hooded man fell to the floor.

Price would have congratulated her, but his reactions

were doing their very best to catch up as it was. He grabbed
the strap of the bag across her chest and with a good amount
of force, he slung her back toward the door.

"Leave now," he yelled.

Price watched a range of emotions pass over her face
amid the growing smoke eking in. It was the only reason
he knew about the incoming attack before he saw it.

Price whirled around, arms up in defense, and blocked
the baseball bat as best he could. Pain slammed into his
forearm. Price couldn't help but yell from it.

The pain and yelling cost him another reaction.

Not JJ.

Without a sound, JJ was back in the fray.

And boy did she make it flashy.

In one fluid movement she seemed to climb the hooded
man like a dang tree. Then she slung herself around until
she was on his back, arm around his throat. The man didn't
like that one bit.

He dropped the bat. Price grabbed it, ready to use it to
end their distraction from escaping the smoke and, no doubt,
growing fire.

Like the entire scene that had played out since spotting
JJ on her run, Price was once again utterly surprised.

With smoke above their heads, a man unconscious near
them on the floor and a siren starting up in the distance,
Price watched as the hooded man propelled himself backward with noticeable force.

That alone wouldn't have been that interesting of a turn
of events.

Yet, he wasn't alone.

Price lunged toward them just as JJ's body connected
against the wall next to the bedroom window.

The sound of the impact was loud enough to hear over the chaos around them.

But JJ didn't make a sound.

Instead, she went limp.

Her body slid like a rag doll off the hooded man as he threw himself clear of Price's lunge forward.

"JJ!"

The only thing Price managed to do was catch her head before it could hit the ground.

It wasn't until he had her securely against him that he realized one problem had just jumped the other.

The fight with the hooded man had ended. He ran out of the bedroom door without a look back.

The fire, however, was just getting started.

STRAWBERRY SHAMPOO.

At first, it was a joke. It smelled so much like an actual strawberry that it was more distracting than refreshing. There they would be, sitting around the dining-room table eating or lounging on the couch watching TV, and the smell of strawberries would mingle in between them. Even in public, the smell was noticeable.

"Who's eating fruit at a football game?" the man sitting behind them at the stadium had asked once.

It was a poignant scent.

Then, one day, it became a part of their family's fabric.

Elle Ortiz was the smell of strawberries, and her husband and daughter began to love strawberries all the more for it.

So that night years ago, JJ didn't need to open her eyes to know her mother was near her. She smelled the strawberries before she smelled the smoke and blood. Before she opened her eyes and screamed. Before she realized her entire life had stopped and she'd never see her parents again.

Strawberries.

It had been nice.

Now, with her eyes closed, she smelled them again.

It's Mom, JJ thought. *She's near me.*

She was pressed against warmth. Moving with their breaths in and out, rumbling against her body as they spoke.

And strawberries.

There was no denying that's what she smelled.

JJ almost smiled.

But then the pain started. It pounded against her skull and radiated down her back. Her elbow ached. Her throat hurt.

Was she back in that car?

She couldn't have been. That had been years ago. It had been raining, it had been night and her godfather had been so loud. Yelling, *screaming* at her to get out. To leave her parents behind. To run and never look back.

Now the sounds were different.

There was a man, but he wasn't yelling. He wasn't trying to scare a little girl into safety.

He wasn't trying to save his best friend's daughter.

Instead, the warmth against JJ had a low rumble. One that was almost soothing.

If she hadn't smelled the strawberries, she might have stayed wondering.

Still, there was enough of a hope that JJ opened her eyes slowly.

The car was supposed to be upside down, her hair and arms were supposed to be hanging down toward the ground, glass and blood across bent metal. The glow from the headlights bouncing off a tree was supposed to show her the outlines of her very still parents and the terrifying and growing cloud of smoke from the engine bay.

However, the world was right side up.

A seat belt wasn't holding her, it was a man. He had her cradled against him like a father would a child, an arm beneath her legs and an arm fastening her upper body to his. He wasn't eerily still like her parents, and he wasn't yelling at her like her godfather. He was speaking softly to someone, somewhere around them.

It was daytime too. Warm even.

There was smoke but it was a good distance off, eating at a house, and not an ominous growing cloud a few feet away.

But.

There *was* the smell of strawberries.

It just wasn't Elle Ortiz's shampoo.

The ache that ran wide and deep, unimaginable in size and depth, filled with a tidal wave of sorrow.

"It's my hair," she said aloud.

JJ's head swam. The body she was attached to moved. Not enough to jostle her but enough to bring her attention to the face peering down at her.

Price Collins was all concern in his eyes.

He didn't understand.

How could he?

She didn't mean to, but the finishing thought slipped out while looking into those eyes.

"It's my shampoo," she said. "Not hers."

Then it was over for JJ.

She placed her head back against his chest and closed her eyes. She was crying next.

"It's okay," Price said. "You're okay. You're okay."

JJ's head swam. She felt nauseous.

The sun overhead bothered her.

She turned her head into Price's shirt and balled her fist into the fabric next to her eye.

He didn't talk to her for a long time or, maybe, it wasn't that long at all. The world felt fuzzy. She felt hungover. She felt drained.

It wasn't until sometime later that Price notably lowered his voice.

"The ambulance is here," he said. "You need to go in it. Who do you want me to call to meet you at the hospital?"

JJ didn't open her eyes. She answered honestly. Her voice had a rasp to it.

"There's no one to call," she said. "I can go alone."

Price made a noise of confirmation. She was about to tell him to let her down, but he started walking.

It wasn't until the ambulance siren was closer that JJ started to come back to the world around them.

"Where's Jamie?" she asked with a start. "Is he okay?"

JJ opened her eyes and found Price's gaze was back on hers.

He searched her expression.

He didn't avoid the question, but his answer was tight. "He's fine."

JJ's eyebrow rose at the way he said it. The small movement made the pain in her head flare. She winced.

"You worry about getting seen to," he added. "Let me worry about everything else."

JJ hadn't known Price long at all.

Yet, for the first time in ages she felt something surprising.

Relief.

Maybe it was because her head was pounding, her elbow hurt something good or she had a sneaking suspicion her back was already black-and-blue, but JJ simply accepted his words.

For now, at least.

Once she found out if Jamie Bell was her brother, then the real work would start for her. And bright eyes or not, she wasn't going to let Price Collins come near the chaos that would come after that.

Chapter Eight

Jamie Bell didn't sustain any injuries from the fire.

Because Jamie Bell wasn't even in Seven Roads.

"He had to change his schedule around last second and go to his new jobsite early to set something up. He was set to come back in the morning before leaving again in a few days."

Price was leaning against the outside wall of the hospital, arms crossed over his chest and nothing but focus on Deputy Little. She had come off patrol duty already but was still hands-on despite the fact that her stomach was growling, and the sun had long since gone down.

But that's just what you had to do when you worked at a department that had less than a football team's worth of employees.

You stepped up because there was space you needed to fill.

"His poor boyfriend Georgie up there was helping him pack up some things when—well, all heck broke loose," Rose said.

This wasn't news to Price. Once they had verified that Georgie Reynolds had been the unconscious man on the floor, Jamie had been called. He'd answered the phone quickly and completely shocked. The brand-new information to Price was the reason behind Jamie being out of town sooner than he'd apparently told others.

"I know you and Miss Shaw left early but I have to say, the fire chief was mighty intimidating at the scene," she added after a moment. "He said we still have to wait for an official report, but he seemed confident, and angry for it, that the gas stove was tampered with to go kaboom. He was surprised there wasn't more damage."

"Something we already suspected, considering there was a whole damn man upstairs ready to fight," Price said. He shook his head. He was angry too. "The way he had Georgie already laid out, it's easy to make the jump that he wanted the fire to spread. We just came in too fast."

Rose nodded. This had been a conversation that they had also already had. The potential plan of the man in the hood and what his motives might have been.

"That's another thing I meant to tell you earlier." Rose snapped her fingers and then pointed at him with a finger gun. "The fire chief made a point to praise your rescue efforts. You managed to get two unconscious adults out of a burning house with little to no injuries yourself." She smirked. "He even said if you're tired of flashing a badge, he'd gladly welcome you into his station."

Rose was trying to lighten the mood. Price knew it and he suspected that she knew that *he* knew it too, because they'd both been present after the ER doctor had sent JJ up for a CAT scan.

To say Price had been angry was an understatement.

He was filled with rage. And not just rage, but rage tinged with guilt.

As smoke had filled the bedroom and neither JJ nor Georgie had moved an inch, Price had known instantly that he wouldn't be able to save both at once. In fact, there was a very good chance that just taking one of them out of the house would be a difficult feat. In his mind, he knew to save one was to most likely damn the other.

He'd already been picking JJ up as the thought blared in his mind.

He carried her through the burning home without hesitation, right out until he was in the backyard and far enough away from the house.

Then, he'd been incredibly lucky to get Georgie out before the fire consumed the walkways and before Price couldn't take the smoke anymore.

By the time he was outside again, some neighbors had converged and were quick to lend a hand. Some took Georgie across the street to wait for the ambulance while the others hurried to make sure neighboring houses were empty, just in case.

One man tried to help with JJ, but Price didn't give him the room.

The second Georgie left his arms, JJ took his place.

Price carried her to the other side of the street as sirens blared in the distance. He kept her there while coworkers and fire fighters converged. He only relinquished his hold once they were loaded into the back of an ambulance.

Now that guilt sat there, reminding him of that split second when Price had thought he was choosing between JJ and Georgie.

It wasn't regret at choosing to take JJ out first. Instead, it was guilt at realizing something he hadn't said aloud.

Once JJ had gone limp against the wall, Price had forgotten entirely that anyone else had existed. Georgie had become an afterthought.

And it shouldn't have been that way.

It was a grating realization. One that was still bothering him.

Rose must have seen the feeling pop up on his expression. She might not have known the exact reason for it but she tried to console him regardless.

"Hey, you did good work today," she said, patting his shoulder twice. "Georgie is going to recover from his fight and our favorite Good Samaritan is too. So try not to worry too much. Instead, do like the sheriff said and get some rest. I know you've gotta be tired."

Price was. His body hurt and the adrenaline had worn off long ago.

But he wasn't going home.

Rose didn't need to know that.

He gave her what he hoped was a nice smile and nodded.

"I'll leave in a bit," he lied. "Let me know if you hear anything, okay?"

Rose said she would, but paused before turning away completely.

"The guy you fought today…do you really think it's the same guy in the mask you fought at Josiah's?" It was a good question. He answered it the same as before.

"The size felt off," he admitted. "But, just because it might not have been the same guy, doesn't mean they aren't working together. The actions are the same at least."

Rose sighed.

"Two violent break-ins and attacks from masked and hooded suspects." She shook her head. Then her gaze went up to the building behind him. "And you and our Good Samaritan JJ have the bad luck to get thrown into the middle of both of them."

She tilted her head a little and let out a brief but heartfelt laugh.

"I gotta say though, that woman up there sure knows how to hold her own," she continued. "If you ever decide to take up the fire chief's job offer, maybe we should ask JJ Shaw to replace you."

Rose said her goodbyes and Price watched her go before walking back into the hospital lobby.

It wasn't until he was in the elevator and pressing the second-floor button that he thought about Jamie Bell's locked back door.

How had JJ opened it so quickly?

JJ DIDN'T HATE HOSPITALS. She just wasn't used to them. At least, not being in them as a patient.

She set herself up on the small couch next to the hospital bed and eyed her IV pole with annoyance. If she hadn't gotten sick in the ambulance—or passed out before—she wouldn't be in this mess. Something she'd already scolded herself for. What was the use of spending half of her life training to withstand almost every hardship, only to be taken out by a wall?

And a man.

Her stomach turned a little. It wasn't because of her confirmed concussion.

Josiah had been attacked.

Jamie Bell's home had been attacked.

Two of the five men who were on JJ's list were coming to, or were already in, the hospital.

It wasn't a coincidence to her anymore.

That meant that JJ had been too slow.

They were finally in town, and they were looking for her brother too.

The question now was: How much did they know?

Had they gone after Jamie Bell because they knew who

he was? Or had they heard that he was about to leave town too and acted like JJ had?

JJ balled her hand into a fist. She made sure not to push down too harshly on her right palm. Along with the scar on her back, there was another just there. Small, but a heavy reminder.

She had been too slow—too careful—in her search for her brother since coming to Seven Roads. It was clear that she wasn't racing against time anymore. She was racing against them.

Him.

And she couldn't lose this time.

JJ's thoughts hyperfocused on everything she knew about her mission. So much so that she almost missed the knock at her door. She must have still looked out of it after inviting them in.

Price's eyebrows drew in, concerned as he walked inside.

JJ mentally pulled herself together, along with the imaginary mask she had been wearing in public since moving to Seven Roads.

She held up her hand to stop his words before he could say what she guessed he would inevitably say.

"Some people don't like hospital food—I don't like hospital beds." She narrowed her eyes at the bed, untouched since she'd been moved out of the ER. "Downstairs, I understood the need to be in one but now I see no point. Especially since I have this handy-dandy rolling IV."

Price's expression of concern turned into a laugh. He wasn't shy about going over to that same bed and patting it.

"Then you won't be offended if I take a load off here for a bit, right?"

He didn't wait for an answer and sat down at the foot of the bed. His long legs nearly reached the ground, but there was a small enough gap between his shoes and the floor that it made for a humorous image. When he swung them a little, JJ felt the urge to smile.

Instead, she took a really good look at the man.

Price had not only ridden with her to the hospital, but he'd also stayed with her in the room she'd been assigned in the ER. Not only had he stayed by her side, he'd done more than just stand there idly.

In the ambulance, he'd held her hair back as she'd gotten sick. In the ER lobby, he had spoken to the front desk clerk to get her checked in. In the room, he'd talked to the attending nurse and doctor, asking more questions than even she had about her own condition.

Price had only left her after she'd been sent to the second floor and *that*, she thought, had mostly been because of her insistence that she was fine and he had more important things to do than babysit her.

It had only been in his absence that she'd felt an itch of disappointment that he wasn't standing next to her.

That itch she'd decided to scratch a second after that thought had come into her head. Staying beneath the radar might have proven useless in the last week or so but she could at least try to stay off Price Collins.

But there he was, swinging his feet while sitting on the edge of her hospital bed, no more than a few feet from her and her IV pole.

He was his usual smiling self.

However, the rest of him seemed to be lagging a bit.

JJ hurt from her fight with the unknown man. She couldn't imagine fighting him and then having to carry two people from a burning house.

He must have been tired and hurting.

She doubted he'd admit it though, just like she doubted she could convince him to leave her alone again.

Maybe if she went a different route this time…

JJ pointed a finger down at his shirt. It was slightly destroyed from the earlier hustle and bustle.

"You know, it might not be a bad idea for you to head home and change into something less almost–flame broiled. I know you said you have a friend who works here, but I've worn her scrubs before, and I don't think they'll fit you."

Price was unfazed. He plucked at his ruined shirt and then shrugged.

"I think this could be a new style trend. Like those jeans with the holes all in the knees that Winnie said was all the new rage. It even has a nice, outdoorsy smell built right in."

He grinned.

JJ retroactively felt bad, once again, for hitting him the week before.

She caught herself from grinning right back.

Instead, she made sure to harden her expression, letting the jolly man know she was serious.

"Listen, I appreciate everything you've done, but you've already done enough. You saved my life—and Georgie's—today. You don't have to hang out with me after. I'm fine."

JJ thought she had finally done it—finally convinced Price Collins to leave—but no sooner had his grin fallen than a look she could only describe as mock offended animated his features.

He even put a hand to his chest in a classic Scarlett O'Hara dramatic move.

"You might be fine, but have you ever wondered about me? What if I'm the one who's not fine?"

JJ opened her mouth. Then she closed it again.

Heat started to crawl up her neck and seep into her cheeks.

Had—had she thought she was special to the deputy? Was his constant consideration only because of his role as law enforcement and not because he cared about her as a—

A friend?

A fellow local?

An acquaintance who had fought alongside him?

JJ didn't know what she would describe their relationship as, and suddenly it left her stumped and in silence.

Thankfully, Price took mercy on her.

He dropped his dramatic pose and gave off a hearty laugh that seemed to fill the room.

"Don't worry, I'm fine too," he said. "I'm just waiting for Winnie and Deputy Gavin to drive my truck here. Then we'll get out of your hair so you can rest."

More than an itch of disappointment moved beneath her skin at that. JJ tried to recover with her own little laugh.

"Well, good then," she said. "I guess waiting in here is nicer than staying in the lobby."

Price's expression did another little change that JJ couldn't track. It was like he had his own mask on, and it slipped enough to see what he was really thinking.

But even that JJ couldn't place.

She wondered if it was simply him being tired.

His next words, however, didn't sound at all like a man in need of his own bed.

He sounded so sure of himself that JJ sat a little straighter as he spoke.

"Staying with you has nothing to do with the lobby downstairs being nice or not. I'm here because you're here."

In all her years of training her emotions to stay hidden, JJ found herself struggling the most right then.

Price Collins might not be dangerous to most, but for her, he was downright a problem.

Chapter Nine

Something was wrong with JJ.

Price knew it—knew it in his bones—but had no right to confront her about it. To ask her what was bothering her. To say he had his finger on *something* but he wasn't sure what. It wasn't just her being uncomfortable in a hospital room. It was *something* else.

But he couldn't say anything of that. All he could do was go along with the plan he'd unknowingly already made the second JJ had admitted she had no one to call to the hospital.

He was going to make sure she wasn't alone.

Not after what she'd just been through.

Which meant another Collins had to be brought into the fold.

"You sure you're okay with this?" Price asked. "You can say no and I won't kick up a fuss."

Winnie had her book bag slung over her shoulder and put on a look that was slightly annoyed.

"I already told you I don't mind," she said. "But if you keep asking me, I'm going to start."

She shook the pillow she had under her arm. He knew there was a blanket and a change of clothes in her book bag too. Winnie handed him the keys to his truck. She kept her voice low as she continued, both trying not to let anyone in the hospital hallway hear their conversation.

Especially not the woman they were talking about in the room behind them.

"I don't mind keeping JJ company while you go home. I like her, remember? So this will be kind of like a sleepover. So don't worry about it."

Price still hesitated.

"I'd stay with her, but I don't think she's comfortable with the idea," he explained again.

Winnie snorted.

"Have you smelled you? I wouldn't want you just chilling in my room while I'm trying to sleep either."

"She's probably not going to be quiet about you staying either," he pointed out. "You might have to do that stubborn thing you do sometimes."

Winnie rolled her eyes and swiped a hand dramatically beneath her chin.

"She was against *you* being here," she said. "Me? I'm a delight."

Price couldn't help but smile.

After he'd gotten to the hospital, he'd made sure to call Winnie's cell and let her know that he and JJ were okay. It was the only part of his job that he'd never liked—worrying her then hearing her try to pretend it didn't.

Even now, between her small jabs, he could see she was straining a little. Just as her hug after arriving had been more tight than normal.

"You're a delight," Price repeated. He meant it.

Winnie dropped her teasing with a nod of her head.

Her expression became serious.

"Go take care of yourself for a change, Dad. We'll be okay."

Price knew enough about himself to understand he would never not worry about Winnie but, in the moment, he accepted that it was time for him to step aside.

At least, for a little while.

That didn't mean he liked it.

"Call me if anything happens," he said. "And regardless, call me in the morning when you're up."

Price didn't say goodbye to JJ for a second time and instead took his truck straight home. There, he did as all three ladies he'd talked to in the last few hours had instructed: he showered.

The water was hot, and it beat against his back without mercy.

It distracted him from his past conversations with Detective Williams and Rose and the sheriff. Then the loop of what-ifs and whys they all had been asking since Josiah Teller's attack. After that, he landed on Good Samaritan JJ, as Rose had started to call her.

There after, and then during, the last two attacks.

Blood on her clothes for both.

A hospital visit after too.

The shower ended and Price wrapped himself in a towel and perched on the edge of his bed.

His back hurt. His whole body hurt.

His ankle hurt too.

If his trip in Jamie Bell's backyard had been worse, it could have been a lot harder to get JJ and Georgie out of that house.

Price tipped backward onto the bed. The intention was to stretch out the soreness radiating through him, then get back up, get dressed and head back to the hospital to wait in the lobby for the morning.

But his intention passed by his follow-through like ships in the night.

Then exhaustion pulled them both under.

PRICE WOKE UP THIRSTY, confused and still in his towel.

It took him several minutes to realize that, not only had he fallen asleep, he had managed to stay asleep for hours. His cell phone's clock let him know it was almost five-thirty in the morning, and no texts from anyone let him know that if anything exciting had happened since his slumber, it wasn't being reported to him.

Price sat up and put his head in his hands. He took a few breaths to try and wake up some more. Instead, he got the nasty reminder that his body had done some more extreme exercises than usual the day before.

He got up and went straight to the bathroom counter. He took two ibuprofen, dressed as fast as he could stand, made some coffee and was headed back to the hospital before five forty-five had rolled around. He was riding the elevator up to the second floor a few minutes later.

And, before six a.m. had a chance to grace Seven Roads, Price was standing outside of a hospital door, looking with concern at JJ Shaw.

The interesting part, however, was the placement of JJ in relation to the hospital door. Instead of being asleep inside of her room, she was standing in the hallway, hovering next to the door. A door that didn't actually lead to her room.

Price gave her a quick once-over—she was still in her hospital gown but no longer attached to an IV pole—before clearing his throat as quietly, but noticeably, as possible.

The noise came through quiet but clear.

JJ whirled around, eyes wide and fists balled.

Price raised his eyebrow at the move. He smiled too.

"I know you said you don't like hospital beds, but staying in hospital hallways is a little extreme, don't you think?"

JJ surprised him with an eye roll. He was glad to see at the same time that she lost some of the tension in her. The fists she had balled opened. She also took a small step toward him and got right to the point before he could ask about it.

"Jamie Bell came in a few minutes ago." She pointed to the door she had been slinking around outside of. "I saw him go in after talking to the doctor, but I couldn't hear what they said."

Price was no longer in a teasing mood.

He stood straighter.

"He hasn't come out yet?" he asked.

JJ shook her head.

"I was hoping to bump into him to ask how Georgie was doing but, well, it hasn't—"

The door they were staring at started to open. JJ was faster. She went from being next to it to next to Price's side. On reflex, he angled in front of her.

They went from looking like eavesdroppers to looking like they were simply going back to her room.

Not that Jamie Bell seemed to mind either way.

The second he caught sight of them, his attention was locked on who they were, not where they were. Once the door clicked shut behind him, he was talking fast.

"Deputy Collins, I was going to try to find you later this morning." He didn't leave JJ out. His gaze shifted to her. "And you? You're JJ, right? They said you'd been admitted but I didn't want to bother you or your daughter until everyone was awake."

Price mentally stumbled over the mention of daughter, then realized that Jamie must have been talking about Winnie.

JJ didn't skip a beat though.

She put a hand on Price's elbow and took a step forward. Her voice changed as she spoke. It was, for lack of a better description, more syrupy.

"We're the ones who didn't want to disturb you." She nodded to the door he'd just come through. "How's Georgie doing?"

Jamie looked like he hadn't slept at all in the last twenty-four hours. His face was haggard.

"He'll make a full recovery. He should be able to go home in the next few days." He paused. A look Price had seen a few times before passed over his expression. Anguish. He met Price's gaze again. "He's my home. Losing the house is hard but losing him would have been…" He shook his head. "Thank you. Both of you for what you did."

Price waved off the gratitude, but JJ answered before he could.

"We're happy to have helped," she said. "And we're glad that Georgie is going to be okay. The whole situation was scary enough without adding a long hospital stay. Speaking of, would you like to grab a quick coffee in the cafeteria with us? They should be open now."

Price was surprised by that but, just as quickly, he was on board.

He knew that Detective Williams had already talked to Jamie, and probably would again now that he was in town, but Price hadn't had the pleasure yet.

And he was mighty curious about a few things.

"It'll be my treat," Price added on. "I'm sure you could use a pick-me-up."

Jamie looked between them and then nodded.

"I wouldn't mind a cup, if I'm being honest."

THE HOSPITAL CAFETERIA was small but there was enough seating that the three of them settled near the entrance to the only public patio. It gave them a big window and a nice view of the sun still rising.

It also helped show that Jamie Bell was, in fact, in deep need of a caffeine boost.

Price felt bad for his plan to pry into the man's already-chaotic affairs.

Jamie, however, dove in first.

"I still can't get over all of this," he said, hands wrapped around his Styrofoam cup as soon as they were seated. "I had just talked to Georgie half an hour before I got the call from the department. Everything had been fine and then suddenly he was unconscious in the hospital and my house had burned down." He shook his head again. "And this guy? The one who broke in? I don't understand it."

Price knew the story of events from Georgie's retelling after he'd regained consciousness an hour after the attack. He had been packing up some things in the upstairs bedroom when the man in the hood had come into the room.

He'd instantly fought with Georgie, and it had been vicious. Georgie hadn't stood a chance and had been laid out quickly.

"I can't even tell if anything was taken," he added. "The house was a total loss."

"And Georgie didn't recognize the man at all?" Price asked.

Jamie shook his head.

"Never seen him a day in his life. And if Georgie hasn't seen him, there's a good chance I haven't either. Other than work, our social circles are the same. And even when it comes to work, I'm a remote worker so the people I interact with are usually not even in state."

There was a sketch artist coming into the department later that day. Price would be giving his account of the man who had attacked them in lieu of Georgie and JJ. He had managed to see just as much of him as the other two. Possibly more, considering he had been fortunate enough to avoid being knocked out.

"So, if this man had picked your house because of you, you wouldn't know why," Price guessed.

"Right," Jamie said.

"Maybe they knew you were out of town and wanted to take something?" JJ offered. She had a small cup of coffee and sat right at his side. Looking down at her, Price couldn't help but feel she resembled a detective at an interrogation table taking on the job of good cop.

Her eyebrows were even drawn together in concentration.

Jamie didn't seem to mind.

"I've already talked about that with Georgie. There's nothing we can think of worth enough for someone to break in and be as vicious as that guy. Definitely not something worth trying to burn my house down over." Jamie looked to Price. "My only valuables are the personal things I usually keep locked up in the closet and, thankfully, Georgie had already moved them to his car before all of this happened."

"Personal things?" Price asked.

Jamie nodded.

"My social security card and birth certificate, a few family and sentimental trinkets, my favorite book signed by the author. Some other odds and ends."

Price felt his eyebrow raise at that.

"You move all of that every time you leave town for work?"

That seemed excessive.

Jamie put on a sheepish look.

"You're not the first person to ask about that." He readjusted the Styrofoam cup between his hands. "I spent some time in foster care when I was a kid, and after being taken from a few homes with little to no notice and nothing but a trash bag to hold everything I owned…well, I've kind of gotten into the habit of taking my most valuables with me when I leave home for too long." He shrugged. "Some people buy safes. I just carry around a cardboard box."

Price felt for the man's past experiences. He was about to point out that it was a trauma response that, at the very least, probably saved his most precious items from the fire, but JJ spoke up.

Her voice was still filled with syrup but surprisingly blunt.

"How long were you in foster care?"

Both men turned to her. She didn't back down.

If Jamie minded past his initial hesitation, he didn't voice it.

"Not as long as a lot of the kids I knew, but from four until around ten. My mom passed and then I was lucky enough to be placed with the Bells, even though I was in a different county."

"I didn't realize that," Price admitted. He knew of the Bells, and had for years. He was older though, never having gone to school at the same time as Jamie.

"Not a lot of people knew at the time, since my parents traveled so much for their work," Jamie said. "It wasn't until I had settled in that they both changed jobs so they were always home." He smiled. He was tired but it was warm. "They made sure to find ways to support me, and even as an adult they still ask for monthly updates on my local adoptees group. I don't have the heart to tell them that we stopped meeting years ago."

"Local adoptees?" There JJ went again. The question was harmless, but Price couldn't help his gut from questioning the tone it came in. It didn't fit but he didn't know how.

Jamie nodded.

"There's a few of us in town still who've been adopted. The Baptist church put the group together when I was in high school. A few of us from it still keep in touch." He addressed Price next. "Josiah Teller was a part of it back in the day too. Him and Nancy Hernandez's sister. The three of us used to be really close."

Price knew Nancy Hernandez.

He knew her sister, Portia, too.

He didn't know Portia had been adopted.

He also didn't care.

Because he had stuck on one thing and one thing only.

Josiah Teller.

Price expected JJ to ask another straight-to-the-point question about Josiah—a man previously attacked after his home was broken into—having a connection with Jamie, a man whose home was broken into and the person inside attacked.

Instead, she didn't say a word.

Price glanced her way.

JJ Shaw wasn't just quiet.

She also wasn't surprised.

It was right then and there that Price felt more than sure of something than he had before.

JJ Shaw was hiding something.

And he had a feeling it might be the reason she was in Seven Roads.

Chapter Ten

They parted ways in the same spot that they'd met. Jamie thanked them a few more times and then went into Georgie's room, yawning despite his coffee.

JJ watched him go.

He wasn't her brother, but she felt sympathy for him.

One moment, his life was going exactly the way he wanted, and in the next, he'd become the man with only a box of valuables left. Though, that sympathy evened out quickly for JJ.

As Jamie said himself, the person he loved would be fine so he would be too.

It was a warming thought that moved through JJ while watching the door close behind him.

That warmth was still there when she turned to Price.

Then it grew cold.

Price wasn't just looking at her. He was staring.

There was a difference.

JJ took a small step back, hunching ever so slightly so her height changed. She also averted her eyes. Hers were a dime a dozen in color but that didn't mean Price couldn't use them to realize she was the one he fought at Josiah Teller's home.

"I'm really glad they'll be okay," she said, swinging her

gaze back to the door behind them. "It definitely could have been a lot worse."

Out of her periphery she saw Price nod. She doubled down on sincerity.

"Speaking of being okay, I really was last night, but I have to say it was nice having someone around. Thanks for getting Winnie to keep me company."

JJ chanced a look at the man.

She could have sighed in relief. He was back to his usual smiling self.

"Hey, I didn't have to force anyone to do anything." He held up his hands in defense. "After you helped me with that man yesterday, she said our family owed you." He shrugged. "And I don't make the rules. I just follow them."

Just as she knew Winnie was a good kid, JJ knew that Price had been the first one to come up with the idea to have someone keep her company. After all, hadn't she admitted to him that she had no one to call?

That didn't seem to be something Price Collins would let sit still.

Friend or not. Acquaintance or not. Whatever-they-could-be-called or not.

Regardless, she had been begrudgingly comforted to have someone to talk to.

Plus, Winnie wasn't like other people in Seven Roads. Her gossip meter seemed to be turned off. That included the power of prying. The teenager didn't ask any questions unless JJ led her to them. Even then, she didn't drill into a topic too long.

It let JJ do something she hadn't done in a while.

She had let down her guard a little.

Now, she remembered that she wasn't dealing with the youngest Collins anymore.

She was back with the big one.

JJ mentally buttoned herself up. She returned his smile.

"I'm also thankful she isn't a snorer," JJ added. "Though she definitely seems to be a deep sleeper. When the nurses did their rounds earlier, she didn't budge."

Price snorted.

"You should see her in the car. If the trip lasts more than ten minutes, she's already been asleep for five."

They quieted as they went into the room, but Winnie was already awake. She had changed out of her pajamas and was making the hospital bed.

"Did you sleep there?" her father asked her.

Winnie immediately pointed to JJ.

"She made me! I told her I'd take the couch, but she was all weird about not liking the bed!"

It was JJ's turn to put her hands up in self-defense.

"I told you I didn't like hospital beds."

Price actually rolled his eyes. The effect was such a drastic softening from the stare she'd just been given. It made JJ wonder if she was being overly paranoid.

It was true that she had been around both break-ins and attacks, but hardly anyone could accuse her of being involved. Only two groups seemed to know the possible connection between Josiah and Jamie.

And it seemed that they had already ruled both men out.

Which meant Marty Goldman might be next.

That's why, instead of staying beneath the Seven Roads radar, JJ had accepted the favor asked of her by Corrie. Marty Goldman would be at the small business networking event that night.

Another reason why JJ was more than ready to leave the hospital, and its beds, behind. Winnie, having already talked about the event the night before, waved her cell phone at JJ and tapped its screen. She was already on the same page.

"I'll text you the hair tutorial link that I talked about when I find it again," she said. "I'm pretty sure it's deep in my Pinterest board but I'll find it before you have to leave tonight. And, again, if Janie from third period can do it by herself and look like she did at last year's homecoming dance, I'm sure you'll really nail it."

JJ smiled at that.

"Much appreciated." She touched her hair. It still smelled softly of smoke. "I'm sure my hair could use the confidence boost."

"Before you leave tonight? You're still going?"

They turned to Price. His carefree attitude was gone again. She had a feeling he was about to give her a speech about taking it easy or more resting, but Winnie stepped in with the assist.

"We already talked about it and decided that JJ could use a little fun after the last week or so," she said. "Plus, it's also for work kind of and if she doesn't go then you'll have to take me and I don't want to be my dad's plus-one. So don't try to talk her out of it."

"The doctor also cleared me during the last round," JJ added in. "He said I'll probably be sore but nothing some Icy Hot or some ibuprofen can't help."

JJ and Winnie were standing almost shoulder to shoulder across from Price now. His gaze moved between them, slow. JJ was momentarily reminded of her own father. She oddly felt like she was also waiting for his approval.

Then, she remembered it wasn't all about her.

Before the fire had broken out, Corrie had changed the plans yet again to include Price as JJ's plus-one to the event. Mostly because he had been unlucky enough to walk inside of the coffee shop after needing a substitute partygoer. Partly because Price seemed to be a man who liked to help out, especially when it was within the realm of his daughter's life.

Since then, neither had had a chance to speak about it though.

JJ felt guilt pulse through her.

"But I definitely understand if you're not feeling up to going," JJ said hurriedly. "You probably are hurting more than me and, well, I guess might need to work overtime? I really don't mind going alone. It's not that far and—"

"I'm going."

Price's words were undeniably concrete.

Three syllables that held power.

Not even his daughter made a quip about it.

Instead, JJ simply nodded.

The rest of their time in the hospital room consisted of packing, going over their schedules for each other and then signing JJ out. There was enough time to take Winnie to school and even a spare twenty minutes to drop JJ off at home before Price had to go to work.

There, in her driveway, Price confirmed his pickup time for that night.

Then, as she was opening the passenger's side door, he threw her off one last time.

"By the way, were you adopted?"

The question came out of nowhere. Normally, that wouldn't matter. JJ had spent years learning how to control her surprise.

Yet, right then and there, she faltered.

"Am I adopted?" she repeated.

Price didn't backtrack the somewhat invasive question. Instead, he explained.

"Yeah. I only ask because you seemed really interested

about Jamie being adopted." A beat went by, then he added, "And Josiah. So, I was just thinking that maybe you might be too."

JJ was lagging.

She felt her smile slide, but she couldn't decide if it seemed natural or not.

She had an entire backstory, locked and loaded for JJ Shaw.

Adopted as a baby by her godfather.

Grew up with him, happy and healthy.

After he married a nice, decent woman and moved up north, JJ decided to come here for a slower pace of life than the city.

She knew what to say and had said it all before.

But there was just something about Price that pulled at her in a way that was wholly uncomfortable.

She wanted to lie; she wanted to tell the truth.

And, for the first time in a long time, she couldn't stop herself from doing both.

"I wasn't, but my brother was."

Price looked like he wanted to say something more, but JJ needed to end the conversation there. So, she did.

"I'll see you tonight, Price."

And with that, she walked away without looking back. If Price wanted more, he didn't get it.

WINNIE TOOK MORE pictures of Price than he had taken of her before the last school dance.

"You're in a suit," she'd said after batting away his complaints. "If I don't document this, then how will future generations know that you had clothes other than your uniform and jeans?"

She'd posed him in front of the fireplace, the bookcase his

father had built by hand, on the front-porch stairs, and—his favorite—looking all dramatic getting into his truck. When he rolled the window down after the photo shoot had ended, she prescolded him for not taking a picture with JJ at the actual event.

"I know you aren't going to do it, but you need to," she had said, finger pointing with purpose. "She already sent me a picture of her hair—which she absolutely nailed—but I want to see the full thing. You two being fancy and awkward at a social event neither one of you wanted to go to."

Price would have normally laughed—said something snarky about being awkward—but he'd spent most of the day at work tired and growing even more so.

The department was frustrated. Price especially.

The sketch artist had come in that morning and done a workup on the man in the hood at Jamie Bell's.

No one had recognized him and, as of that afternoon, nothing had popped in any of their law enforcement databases for him.

Detective Williams had said he had a potential lead, but hadn't been back to the department all day.

Then there was the part of Price that had branched off during his idle time and done a little digging himself.

Both Jamie and Josiah had in fact been adopted. Though, at different ages and in different circumstances. Before, during and after the legal paperwork had been done, they had seemingly led completely separate lives other than the occasional support group meeting.

That, and their attacks, would have been enough to draw his attention.

But then Price had seen another similarity that he couldn't ignore.

Josiah Teller and Jamie Bell were the same age.

"That was one reason our parents really wanted us to see each other," Josiah had said on the phone earlier. Price had called to check up on him but also to mention his conversation with Jamie the day before. "They thought we could relate more to each other since we were in the same grade too. Everyone else in the group was younger or older by a few years."

After that, Price couldn't help but pivot to JJ.

Her social media presence was barely there and, of the accounts, there were no family ones attached. Price started to put her name into a more involved search but stopped himself again.

Just because JJ was hiding something didn't mean it was his business.

It didn't mean it was bad.

Price held onto that thought with new resolve. He held it fast as he parked at the curb outside of her house and then went to the front door to knock. He held it true as he waited for her to open the door.

Then he didn't have to work hard at all to keep his thoughts from wandering.

Price didn't know much about hair tutorials or fashion, but he believed in that moment that JJ Shaw had indeed nailed it.

The dress code for the event was cocktail; JJ Shaw was devastating.

She wore a black dress that cut above the knees, dipped down the chest and matched up nice with a pair of ankle boots. There was a small leather jacket hung over one of her bare arms, and the purse she wore across her body had a gold chain the same color as the hoops in her ears.

As far as hair went, his daughter had pulled through. Half of it was pinned back in a braid, the rest curled and falling across her shoulders like some kind of movie star readying for a premiere.

JJ caught his reaction easy enough.

She smiled uncertainly.

There was no recovering.

"I think I might be underdressed."

JJ waved her hand at him.

"Stop it. Don't go making me feel any more self-conscious than I already do. Corrie already made me video chat while I was getting ready and that was enough to make me rethink going at all." Price stepped back as she started to shut the door behind her. She stopped and patted at where a pocket might have been had her dress had one. "Ugh. Speaking of, I left my phone in my room. Let me grab it really quick."

She turned, jacket still over her arm, and stepped back into the house.

That's when he saw it.

A scar shone across a stretch of JJ's back, uncovered by her hair that had parted just so.

Scars were nothing new to Price. He'd seen his fair share—big and small and everything in between—and even had a few of his own.

Yet, maybe it was because he'd already felt off about the woman, this scar seemed different.

It seemed angrier than most he'd seen before.

And he had a feeling JJ hadn't wanted him to see it.

Her jacket was on when she came back but Price took extra care not to glance down regardless. He also worked to keep their small talk on the drive to the venue in the city away from any topics that were less than ideal. A move that she also seemed okay with following.

They talked about the coffee shop, about Corrie and her sister Cassandra, and touched on some fun stories about

Winnie as a little kid. No one went deeper than that and talk about the recent violent attacks stayed out of the cab of the truck entirely.

When they parked across the street in the public lot from the venue, that small talk went to a plan of action for them to do their best at networking for the Twenty-Two Coffee Shop.

"Are you ready?" Price asked, holding his arm out once they had made their way to the outside of the building. There were a few other guests coming up behind them, also dressed to impress. He could also hear the consistent chatter of several people inside.

JJ nodded.

There were no nerves showing from her.

Instead, she seemed oddly focused.

If Price had known that the next time he'd come back through the doors, everything would be different, he might have changed his mind.

But there was no way to know.

So, he held onto JJ and went inside with a smile, oblivious to the domino effect they were about to set in motion.

Chapter Eleven

The gathering was a lot more upscale than JJ had originally thought it would be. Business owners, operators, investors and some leading industry-specific professionals all mingled around a ballroom while waiters and waitresses moved in-between with actual trays of drinks and appetizers balanced on their hands.

JJ was immensely glad that she had listened to Corrie, who had suggested she go dressier rather than the blouse and slacks she had originally intended to wear. She wasn't the only one.

Price lowered his chin over her shoulder. His name tag brushed against her jacket. She could feel his breath at her ear.

"Remind me to give Winnie a raise in her allowance next month. I would have worn jeans if it wasn't for her."

JJ stilled herself from reacting to the closeness. She did smile though.

"Sounds good to me. I owe her for the hair anyway."

Price pulled two drinks from a waiter as they glided by and stood tall at her side once distributing them. He took in a deep breath and then nodded.

"Okay, so the plan is to find the florist lady Cassandra and Corrie want to get in good with, right? And then rub elbows with the local event lady."

He bobbed his head around. It wasn't as noticeable as it might have been had the room not been filled with tables, chairs, standing decorations and enough guests that the live music at the back of the room was competing with their chatter.

"Robertson. Maggie Robertson," JJ reminded him. "Cassandra wants to start hosting events at the coffee shop and thought if we were friendly enough with her, we could do some kind of partnership deal in the future."

Price nodded. His eyes continued to scan the room.

JJ was doing more of the same.

However, she wasn't looking for Maggie Robertson or the head of the local event scene.

She was looking for Marty Goldman.

"The picture Corrie gave you isn't helping me here," Price said after a moment. "We need to move around so I can start reading name tags too."

JJ felt a small pressure at her lower back as Price gently placed his hand there. He pushed a little. It put JJ in step beside him.

Once again, JJ struggled to rein in her focus.

"I'll let you start the conversations, but let me know if you get tired of schmoozing and I'll jump in," he whispered, oblivious to her mental stumble. "Or I can help you escape if you need instead. I'm really good at diverting conversational attention."

Somehow, JJ didn't doubt that. With one hand and a slight push, he'd managed to divert her attention and scatter her thoughts.

If Price Collins put his mind to actively being distracting?

JJ let out a little laugh.

"Pick a code word and I'll be sure to say it."

Price nodded. She glanced over to see a smile had tugged up the corner of his lips.

"Let me think on it a bit. It has to be a good one."

For the next half hour, they weaved in and out of party-goers, stepping into ongoing conversations and then starting their own. Everyone had business cards and together JJ and Price became a well-oiled machine in presenting the one from the coffee shop and accepting cards from the people they were networking with. Price also took it upon himself to put each in the pockets of his suit. It was a move that JJ found oddly touching.

They ebbed and flowed like that in a comfortable rhythm, despite not sighting either one of their targets, including Marty Goldman.

"Maybe they're some of those people who like to be fashionably late or just have to make a dramatic appearance," Price reasoned as they took a water break next to one of the caterer tables. "We can keep schmoozing around until we see one of them or try to get someone more exciting on our side."

He looked absolutely mischievous as he openly scanned the crowd near them. He was covert when he nodded toward the group of people milling closer to the band.

"That guy there? The one with the brown suit and lady half his age on his arm? I'm pretty sure that's the guy who runs the courier service the art lady we talked to last said was a good person to know. Why don't we go accidentally bump into him?"

JJ agreed but, as they started walking that way, she had to scold him a little.

"What is it with you and not learning names? I'm not sure I've heard you say a name other than *that man* and *that lady*."

Price fell back a little as a group walking by forced him to slow down. It put JJ a few steps ahead of him. Still, she imagined his expression. He was probably smiling, laughing a little and ready to lob a cheeky remark back. JJ realized she was almost looking forward to turning to him once there was more room to see if she was right.

But she didn't get the chance.

She had found something familiar in the ballroom.

Her feet kept going a few steps, unsure if her eyes really were seeing what they thought they were.

Who they thought they were.

There was no way, absolutely no way that her old life was here.

Not like this.

Not with the two of them.

The men were in suits, standing on the outskirts of the group of people watching the live band play. One wore a comfortable-looking fit, dark blue and complimenting his blond hair. The other had a suit that was classic. Black, white button-up, a tie that was plain but no doubt expensive. His hair was copper. His resting smile was sharp.

While both men were together in the same space, sharing a conversation, they were light-years from each other.

One was Marty Goldman, suit blue.

The other was the son of the man who had killed JJ's family.

Her instincts tore themselves apart. JJ took another step forward and then stopped.

If it had been anyone else at Marty's side…

Was he here for Marty?

Surely, he was.

Why else would he be talking to him of all people…

Was this the first time they had met?

What was his plan next?

Did that mean Marty was her brother?

The ballroom seemed to become silent around her. Then it was an echo chamber of nothing but questions. None of them she could answer.

Then those questions came to a screeching halt as a sight that truly terrified her took place.

The two men started to walk away from the crowd, heading in the direction of side doors that led deeper into the building.

Josiah Teller had been viciously attacked in his own home, driven away and then dumped in a field. Jamie Bell's house had been partially blown up, then absolutely destroyed all while the sole occupant had been beaten and left to the same fire.

What would happen to Marty Goldman if he wasn't the son of Able Ortiz?

What would happen if he was?

"The last dance I went to was the father-daughter one for Winnie when she was in middle school, but I'm sure I can pull out a few moves that won't embarrass you too badly."

Price's voice filled the terrifying silence that had wrapped around her. She hadn't realized they had made it to the small stretch of dance floor other guests were currently using. A couple moved smoothly past them, but JJ was still eyes on Marty, moving farther and farther away.

JJ didn't have time to wonder why she did what she did next.

Instead, all of her seemed to come up with a new plan right on the spot.

One that finally included another person.

JJ spun around and took Price's hand in hers. When she

spoke, her voice was low but had years of pain, anger and determination powering through every word.

"I'm about to give you a lot of information and there's no time to ask questions about it, but I promise I'll explain more later. Right now, I need your help."

Price had been smiling.

That smile disappeared.

She didn't wait for the go-ahead.

She went for the jugular instead.

"My real name is Lydia Ortiz, and I moved to Seven Roads to try and find my biological brother before the people who killed my parents find him." She touched her chest with her free hand. "I'm the person you fought in Josiah Teller's house, but I am not the one who hurt him, and I am not working with the man who hurt Georgie. The man who most likely did is walking away with Marty Goldman right now."

She moved her hand so she was pointing to Marty's retreating back.

The doors were already closing behind him. She couldn't even see the black suit his companion wore anymore.

It pulled her anxiety as high as it could go.

She had run out of time.

If Price wasn't going to help, she hoped he wasn't going to stop—

"What do you need from me?"

His words came out calm and even. His expression was impassive.

JJ didn't question either.

"I need you to be a distraction."

THE SOUNDPROOFING OF the doors was impressive. As soon as they closed behind Price, it was like he had stepped into an entirely different world.

It was quiet, for one. Not even the thump of the music behind him penetrated through. The same went for those chatting inside. Instead, Price only heard lowered voices and footfalls from the few guests who were walking to and from their destinations.

No one was stopping to chat.

That went double for Marty Goldman and the man in the black suit.

They weren't wasting time to get to wherever they were going. Price was surprised at the distance between him and the two already.

He wasn't the only one.

JJ had followed him into the hallway. He couldn't see her but felt her tucked back at his flank.

JJ.

Lydia.

Price didn't have time to sort out the bombshell she'd just dropped on him.

The only truth he knew and accepted was her belief that Marty Goldman was in danger and that the man in the black suit was the danger.

He wasn't going to let that instinct go simply because he couldn't see the whole picture he was apparently now a part of.

It helped that the more he closed the distance between him and the two men, the more he could tell something was wrong with them.

Marty, a man he knew by name and had seen a few times around town, was walking like a man who'd had too much to drink. There was an unevenness to it. A tilt. Barely there but like his body and brain couldn't decide what either were supposed to do.

Go fast? Slow down? Stop? Run?

The man at his side, though, was the complete opposite.

He knew where he was going and just how he was getting there.

His gait was smooth, his clip even.

But where were they headed?

The hallway stretched the length of the building, only turning right into the rest of the paths and rooms in the convention center. Straight ahead, the hallway dead-ended into a window that stretched from floor to the two-story-high ceiling.

Was there another event happening deeper inside?

Or were they taking the exit to the outdoor area?

Maybe they were going to the bathrooms instead?

JJ slipped her hand into Price's, pulling his attention enough to include her in it.

Her voice was a whisper next to his shoulder.

"Marty is panicking. Look at his shoulders."

Price had been so focused on Marty's walk that he hadn't taken in the set of his shoulders.

She was right. They were stiff as a board, held high and rigid.

Not the look of someone who had had too many drinks and was being helped to the bathroom.

Then the first turn into a hallway happened. The men turned but had to step around an elderly couple walking in the opposite direction. It gave the man in the suit enough space to cut his gaze their way.

JJ's hand disappeared from Price's grasp.

"He can't see me," she said urgently.

Price didn't think she had to worry about that.

The man in the suit made eye contact with Price and Price alone.

And they both held the gaze longer than they should have.

"Don't follow us," Price ordered, body already tensing in anticipation.

"What?"

Price undid the button holding his suit jacket closed.

"We've got a runner."

JJ repeated the question, but the man proved Price right. He ran, disappearing completely from view.

Price was right behind him.

Chapter Twelve

Marty Goldman slid into JJ's view as Price disappeared from it.

JJ ran to the man she could see, stopping next to Marty with her hands flitting around the air above him in worry.

"Are you okay?" she yelled at him.

Marty looked the part. Sure, he was disheveled and seemed panicked, but there were no obvious signs of trauma or blood.

He confirmed with a nod.

"Yeah, I'm—"

JJ spun around on her heel and was charging after Price before he could finish his sentence.

The hallway wasn't as long as the previous one. Instead, it branched off several times before coming to its end. JJ had already lost sight of Price by the time she skidded to a stop at the last option to turn. She listened for a few beats.

Then she heard a door slam somewhere in the distance.

JJ backtracked and followed the echo to what seemed to be the main hallway. There was an elevator at its end, another door for the stairwell next to it. JJ didn't have to open it to know that's where they had gone. She could hear the loud footfalls hitting what must have been metal and concrete.

JJ did some quick math.

They were probably ahead of her by one flight. If she ran in after them, not only would she be unable to catch up, she would be in danger of exposing herself as involved.

What would the man in the black suit do?

Would he get off at the first floor he could, or try to put more distance between Price and himself?

There was no time to sit and wonder.

So, she left it up to fate.

JJ smashed the up button for the elevator. If the doors opened in the next few seconds…

They opened immediately.

JJ tucked inside and decided to press the second floor. Her painted fingernail was backlit by the lit up Two but her mind was already in planning mode a floor above. If she was fast enough, maybe she could catch sight of them if they had left the stairwell. If not, she would go up another floor.

The sound of someone coming made her move her finger on reflex to the close-door button. However, the person was faster. He swept into the elevator and turned to face the doors in one fluid move.

JJ was about to stumble her way through, making an excuse that would get him to leave, when she realized who exactly he was.

JJ didn't know why she even made plans.

Fate sure didn't let her keep them.

Lawson Cole wore his black suit well. There was no doubt about it. Up close, she could see that it was also, in fact, tailored specifically to him. Like a second set of skin. It didn't look like he was a man who had been asked to dress up and attend an event. Instead, he looked like a man the event had been thrown for.

It was infuriating to see him doing so well.

It was terrifying to see him so close.

And it was worrying that Price didn't come into view as the elevator doors closed in front of them.

JJ assessed the situation as fast as she could. Lawson wasn't making any quick movements. He hadn't grabbed her or said her name or even, it seemed, looked at her.

Had he not seen her running behind him and Price?

Maybe he thought she was just some partygoer who was exploring or a staff member on business?

JJ took a tentative step back.

The doors might have opened quickly, but she had severely misjudged the speed of the actual elevator. It hadn't even started rising yet.

If Lawson hadn't recognized her, would it be suspicious for a normal person to just stand there motionless without speaking?

Or this is the time, a thought said, skittering across her mind. *You could confront him now and end this.*

But it wouldn't end this, would it?

Could it be that simple?

And where was Price?

She couldn't simply expose herself, attack Lawson and expect the deputy to be okay with it all.

The elevator finally started to rise.

JJ decided to feign innocence.

"Oh, I'm sorry. Which floor did you want?" She didn't turn her face toward him but instead motioned to the panel. "I have a phobia of elevators and kind of forget to be present when I'm in them."

She did a little laugh. Polite, self-deprecating.

Lawson surprised her by doing more of the same.

"The second floor works for me too," he replied with a laugh.

JJ assumed he hadn't seen her running. She assumed *he* assumed that she hadn't seen him running either. She could play this off until they parted ways.

Then she could follow him.

From there she could make a new plan.

From there she could—

"Elevatophobia."

JJ inclined her head a little.

The rising had slowed. The doors still weren't open though.

"Huh?"

"That's the name for it," Lawson said. "The phobia of elevators is *elevatophobia*."

The hit that came next was brutal, and JJ couldn't dodge even a fraction of its power.

One second they were facing the front of the elevator, and the next she was pressed against the back of it, a hand around her neck.

JJ's own hands flew to Lawson's in an attempt to cut off the contact. But Lawson's grip was phenomenal. JJ coughed as he squeezed.

"If you didn't like elevators, you shouldn't have gotten into this one." It came out as an almost-purr. To match, his grin became catlike. "You're here to help the deputy, and now you're going to help me instead."

JJ could move her body fine but the force he had on her neck had her completely at his mercy with no plan to counterattack.

She curled her fingernails into his skin, but Lawson looked as if he'd already lost interest in her. He turned his head to look behind him.

"I thought he might be around here."

He moved enough that JJ was able to see that the elevator doors had finally opened. A small open area gave way to a hallway that looked to run between several rooms. Half of the lights were turned off.

Movement came out of one of those areas, heading straight for them at a slow but even clip.

JJ met Price's eye.

The sound of a grin was still in Lawson's words.

"Stop or I'll break her," he said.

To show he meant it, he tightened his grip. JJ couldn't help but let out a strangling cough.

Price stopped dead in his tracks.

He wasn't grinning but his words were just as sinister.

"Let her go or I'll break *you*."

Lawson must have believed him. His grip didn't detract but it did loosen.

"Prove to your date that you can breathe," he ordered. "Say something."

Your date.

Lawson was referring to her as Price's date.

Not as Lydia Ortiz.

He didn't recognize her.

He didn't know her.

That meant he couldn't *really* use her.

Every fear, every hesitation that JJ had fallen prey to since the reappearance of Lawson Cole felt like it dripped down from his hand and melted into a puddle on the floor.

If he didn't know her, then he'd already underestimated her.

JJ's face must have given away her change in mindset. Price's brow drew in together.

She complied with Lawson's order and spoke to him.

It just wasn't what either man had apparently been expecting.

"I'm actually really good at fighting."

Price's eyebrow rose and Lawson started to turn to face her.

JJ was already moving.

THE WOMAN DROPPED her body weight out of nowhere.

Lawson caught a glimpse of her smile before he had to release his hold on her neck. That glimpse lasted as long as a blink. There was no time to do anything but defend after that.

Now in a low crouch, she threw an elbow that buried deep within his side. It was a biting, sharp pain that made him stagger back into the corner of the elevator. His hand hit the panel to try and steady himself. He only had a split second to decide to use the misstep to his advantage.

He pressed one of the upper floor's numbers along with the close-door button.

Then the woman was back on him.

He caught a punch she was throwing only to take a kick in its place. It went into his hip but not his groin. That would have spelled disaster. Especially with the deputy on the outskirts.

Lawson needed to at least keep him away from the fray.

He took the woman's hand still in his grip and slung her against the opposite wall. It gave him a small window to deal with the approaching brawn of the deputy.

In a hit that felt movie-worthy, he connected a powerful blow against Deputy Collins's chest. If it had connected with his head, it would have been a knockout. Instead, all it could do was literally knock the man back.

He tried to catch himself, but he hit the floor hard.

The doors started to close. He wasn't going to make it.

But his date?

She was an absolute nuisance.

"Fifth floor," she yelled out.

Then the doors closed.

Lawson managed to move as the woman used the wall to push herself at him like a spring. She ducked as he swung out and got him again in the side. Before he could recover, she swept out with one leg and nearly pulled one of his along with it.

But they were in a small area, and he was a tall man.

He used the walls to his advantage to keep himself upright.

The momentary win let him switch to offense.

When the woman came at him again, he returned the side jab with one of his own.

It landed.

She let out a yell of pain and stopped her onslaught, trying to backpedal.

He wasn't going to let her.

Lawson struck out again, this time aiming to get her in a chokehold where he would certainly apply more pressure than before.

Yet, the woman surprised him once more.

Instead of the attack landing or her avoiding it all together, she used it.

Catching his wrist with one hand, she used the other to send a hit to the outside of his elbow. The pressure applied the wrong way to the bend of his arm was shockingly painful. Lawson forgot his earlier plan of attack and yelled as his reflexes had him trying to get more to his right to ease the pain.

The move created a perfect opening for the woman.

He heard her heel connect with the metal of the elevator wall while she jumped up and moved around and onto his back. Her hold went from a hand on his wrist to her arm around his neck.

Now he was the one in a chokehold.

It was impressive, objectively speaking.

It might have worked had it been someone else.

But Lawson wasn't afraid so there was no reason to panic.

He coughed as his air supply was cut off but kept the rest of his body in motion.

He reached back and grabbed the woman's jacket.

Then he yanked her off and slung her away like a wet shirt.

Skills were nice but his size wasn't something she could ignore.

The woman made a noise as she hit the floor.

He knew by that sound that it had hurt.

"I don't think your guy is worth all of this," he grunted out to her, rubbing at his neck.

Lawson had to give it to the woman. She had spirit.

She scrambled to her feet and hurried backward so she was opposite him, the corner behind her. Despite being in a dress that didn't seem too comfortable and boots with a noticeable height, she fell into another fighting stance.

The elevator was slowing.

He had no doubt Deputy Collins would meet them when those doors opened.

Lawson couldn't go another round with this woman or her date.

He needed to finish what he'd come to do. Seeing the deputy had already been a complication. He didn't need any more than he already had.

So Lawson pulled out the knife that security had missed. It was small, thin, but undeniably effective.

And the woman must have realized it. Her stance went from attack to defense, her forearms raising slightly so she could cover her face if she needed to quickly.

Something Lawson wasn't keen on testing at the moment.

He spelled it all out for her.

"You might be able to get some hits in on me, but with this, no matter how good you are, I'll be able to return the favor." He shook the knife. "And this will hurt a whole lot more than fists."

The woman didn't say he was wrong.

She also didn't test his theory. She stood there in silence as the elevator doors opened again.

"Good to see you again, Deputy," Lawson said in greeting to the panting deputy outside of the doors.

He eyed the weapon and then glanced at his date.

Lawson didn't want to waste any more time. He pointed to the woman.

"Get out," he growled. "Or I'll shred both of you."

If looks could kill, Lawson believed his time would have come to an end right then and there. Yet, the woman didn't have the power. Instead, she shared a look with the deputy.

He nodded.

Only then did she slowly move along the wall and out of the elevator. Not one moment of that did she break eye contact with Lawson.

He had to hand it to her. She had been an interesting opponent.

Lawson turned the knife out and stood just inside of the elevator doors. The deputy moved but only to put himself in front of his date.

His stare was just as unrelenting as Lawson pressed the button for the first floor and then the close-door one next to it.

Lawson was glad to see that the deputy had enough sense to keep his position as the doors slowly started to close, but there was obviously something he wanted to say.

It just wasn't at all what Lawson had expected.

"Marty Goldman was born from an affair. His parents lied. He isn't adopted."

Lawson's head tilted in question just as the doors closed.

The ride to the first floor was faster than it had been on the way up.

Lawson made quick work of exiting it, and the building, without any issues.

It wasn't until he was being driven away that he let himself sit with his thoughts.

After a few minutes he turned to the man sitting beside him in the back seat.

"Marty Goldman might not be adopted. It might have been a lie his parents told to cover up an affair."

"Is that why you didn't grab him?" the man asked.

Lawson didn't want to go into detail.

"Find out if it's true."

The man nodded. He wasn't in a position to ask too many questions. It was his fault Lawson had gone into public in the first place after his botched attempt to get Josiah Teller.

Lawson ran a hand through his hair.

He spied a rip in his suit jacket's sleeve.

He'd already not been a fan of Deputy Collins since his involvement in their Jamie Bell search. And now? Now he was around Marty Goldman?

It looked like the deputy had caught on to their common thread.

Not that he was too surprised. It wasn't like there were that many men from Seven Roads of the same age and adopted.

Still, the deputy sure had become surprisingly annoying.

Not to mention his woman.

Lawson noted the various pains she had inflicted on him.

He decided then and there that before this was over, he would teach them both a lesson.

And his mantra?

Ladies first.

Lawson pulled the name tag that had fallen off inside of the elevator out of his pocket and handed it to the man next to him.

"I also want you to find out everything you can on JJ Shaw."

Chapter Thirteen

Lawson was nowhere to be found. Security didn't see him and the cameras around the convention center were of no help. The fact that there had been none in the area where they had fought Lawson definitely was a blow to Price's mood.

As was Marty Goldman's apparent lack of information about the man.

"He said he was one of the investors from a group I've been trying to get in touch with," he'd told JJ and Price once they confirmed he was absolutely fine. "He said he could get me into his higher ups' good graces if I could pitch my newest idea to them here. I—I didn't have any of my notes or information, but I couldn't pass up the opportunity."

So the panicked Marty they had seen had been because of business, not safety.

He wasn't JJ's brother, but she couldn't help but feel sisterly and scold him.

"Next time a stranger asks you to come with him to a secluded place, don't," she'd said.

Marty, to his credit, looked sorrowful for his error in judgment. He made another one as he accepted her lie that she believed the man had been a scammer, ready to take his money.

Price, in hearing this, followed up with such a serious warning that both she and Marty had snapped to attention.

"If you ever see or hear from him again, immediately call me."

Marty had agreed to the terms and JJ had lightly suggested he keep what happened quiet. Since he had been the one to wander off with a stranger and, in his mind, nearly get robbed, it was a concession he was more than willing to make.

After that, Price had simply turned to JJ and said four words that zipped her mouth shut tight.

"We're going home now."

The drive back took place in stony silence.

JJ didn't know how she should break it. Or, really, what she should break it with. Price not enlisting the authorities for Lawson had been a surprise. Him not driving her directly to the department once they were back in Seven Roads? Also a surprise.

One she was glad to meet as they parked in the driveway.

Price's driveway.

"Winnie is staying the night at a friend's house," he announced. "Let's go."

His tone was sharp but not particularly loud. JJ didn't like the change from the happy-go-lucky man she had grown used to seeing. Then again, she had been the reason for the change.

She watched him exit the truck and walk around the hood.

He didn't even look back at her as he went and started to unlock the front door.

I could run right now, JJ thought. *There's only two more names and now I know Lawson's here. I don't have to keep playing pretend. I can just hide.*

JJ opened her door and then closed it softly behind her.

He may know who I am but if I wanted to, I could disappear from his life forever.

She walked up the sidewalk and paused as he opened the door.

I can do all of this alone. I don't need him.

JJ followed Price into his home.

She didn't have the mental bandwidth at the moment to think about why, for the first time ever, she was deciding to trust someone.

Instead, she let her instincts take over.

And, for whatever reason, they were at ease around Price Collins.

"Are you hurt anywhere?"

Price's voice broke through her thoughts with a start.

JJ shook her head.

"Nothing but bruising." She tapped her side. "He only landed one hit and, thankfully, it was this side." JJ stopped herself from adding that it was a lucky hit, considering she had just recovered from Price's rib shot during their fight at Josiah's. She cleared her throat and motioned to his chest.

"What about you? He slugged you pretty good from what I saw."

Price's face was impassive. She couldn't read a thing on it.

"I'm fine," he answered. "Want some water?"

"I'm good," she said.

"Good."

He walked off like the conversation was over. JJ couldn't help but raise an eyebrow as she followed him into the living room to the right. Its decor was rustic and warm, covered in knickknacks and walls with framed pictures of Winnie and him through the years. If she had been there under different circumstances, JJ would have liked to have taken a closer look at everything.

Instead, Price motioned to the couch.

No sooner was JJ sitting then he brought over a dining room chair. He sat it opposite her, a small coffee table between them, and then settled onto its seat.

Then those bright eyes of his were zeroed in on only her.

"It's time you explain."

JJ didn't know what she expected.

Still, she found herself tamping down the urge to sigh.

Price had saved her life in the fire. At bare minimum he deserved her respect.

So, she started at the beginning without any more hesitation.

"My dad used to work for the FBI, dealing with white-collar crime cases in the South. *His* father had been conned out of all their family savings when he was a kid and, because of it, they had a lot of rough years." JJ adjusted in her seat. She hadn't told this story to anyone and now, even though she was okay to tell Price, she felt wholly uncomfortable for it. "But that made my dad work all the harder to help others avoid the same fate. So, he didn't just do his work. He made sure he was really good at it."

JJ wanted to smile for her father reaching his life's dream. She only stopped herself because of the nightmare that had followed.

"When I was really little, there was this anonymous group of men in suits that fit the kind of criminal my dad went after. They cropped up in Tennessee and really started becoming a problem. That wasn't my dad's jurisdiction, but he followed the case like a football fan might follow a team's schedule until eventually he met a man named Riker

Shaw, an agent working the case. They became fast friends and, eventually, Riker became my godfather."

Price didn't stop her here, like she thought he might.

Instead, he kept listening with obvious rapt attention.

JJ continued, not exactly wanting to say what happened next but knowing she needed to do it all the same.

"A few years later, a branch of that anonymous group had popped up around Georgia and, finally, in my dad's jurisdiction. By that point, he and Riker had become almost experts on the group, so Dad was the point person here."

JJ smiled a little. She pointed to the wall behind Price but envisioned the city they had just come from.

"We actually didn't live too far from Seven Roads when I was a kid," she said. "In fact, before everything, I had been here a few times with my mom. She had a few friends we would occasionally visit. It was when I was younger though. And it was before the accident."

JJ let out a quick breath.

Price's bright eyes kept on shining on her.

"My dad was apparently finally able to get enough information on the group that he wasn't just about to shut down the branch, but cut down the entire tree," she continued. "It was big news. News that he and Riker realized had reached the wrong people. So, one night, Dad loaded me and Mom up and had us racing to a safe house where Riker was going to meet us. We didn't make it."

The small moon-shaped scar on her palm felt hot. JJ knew it wasn't. She knew the mark her fingernails had bit into her hand were old and worn.

Still, she had to fight the urge to rub at it. To try and smooth it away.

Because the ache in her definitely wasn't going anywhere.

"A man chased us down and drove us off the road. It was raining so the accident, which might not have been so bad, was fatal."

She could see Price; she could see her parents hanging motionless upside down in front her.

"I was the only one who woke up," she said, keeping her voice as even as possible. "I had no idea what was going on but then there was Riker, yelling at me to get out."

JJ couldn't help but pause here.

She admitted something to him that she truly had never wanted to say aloud before.

"I'll never forget the face he made after he checked on my parents and then looked back at me. I knew it then. They were gone. They were gone but it also wasn't done. The bad guys were still coming."

JJ took in a breath. She didn't pause anymore.

"Riker didn't get me too far, despite his best efforts. We were caught by two men, and, weirdly enough, we were lucky that one of them was the actual leader of the group. A man named Jonathan Cole."

Price's eyebrows pulled together.

"Any relation to our friend Lawson Cole from the elevator?" he asked.

She nodded.

"Jonathan was his father. And, let it be known right now, Lawson is nothing like his father." She leaned forward a little and held up two fingers. "Jonathan had only two rules that he made sure no one broke, no matter what scheme or activity they were running. That was you don't hurt women, and you don't hurt children. No matter what."

"Chivalrous," Price commented.

She nodded.

"And the only reason why the Ortiz children are alive."

JJ put the fingers down and started to rub at her palm. "Jonathan struck up a deal with Riker right then and there. If Riker didn't release the evidence, Jonathan would keep the secret that not everyone had died in the car accident. He would also cover our tracks until we could leave our lives behind and start new ones. Riker, a single man who had never dreamed of having a family and then suddenly had a ten-year-old to look after, took the deal. We left, got new identities, and have lived as father and daughter ever since with no trouble ever coming our way.

"I had a good childhood with Riker. I really did. He gave me the world and really did become a second dad to me. He also helped me work through a lot of emotions that I struggled with, about knowing my dad's killers were just out there. I even thought for a bit that I had moved on as much as I could. But then Jonathan Cole himself visited me last year."

This was where JJ's emotions fluctuated a bit.

This part was new.

Price's eyebrow rose. JJ still couldn't forget her own surprise when she had seen the old man for the first time since she was a kid.

"Apparently, he had known for a while where I was but had kept his promise through the years. He'd worked hard to not let anyone know that there had been survivors in the accident. He saved a life to pay for his man taking a life, is what he'd said. The only problem was, he'd kept the secret too well. He didn't even tell us that my mother had also survived. So we had no idea that she was pregnant."

This part undeniably hurt. JJ had to speak in facts not emotions or she'd be crying soon. Telling Price had been hard enough. Losing it on his couch…that would be too much.

And she couldn't afford that right now.

Her words came out cold for her effort. She muscled through them the best she could.

"Jonathan said he never told her that I had survived either and so, thinking she lost her entire family, she accepted the protection he gave her and hid away from the world throughout her pregnancy. Then, when the time came to give birth, she had several complications. They continued to be an issue months after my brother was born and she passed away before he turned one."

Despite her best efforts, a lump formed in JJ's throat.

She would never know the end of her mother's life, and it tore at her soul to think of her going through everything by herself.

It was one reason finding her brother had become everything to her.

JJ clenched her hand into a fist. She eased it out in the next moment.

"Jonathan said he purposely lost track of my brother after that, thinking that knowing anything more than a general location would put him in danger. All he knew was the town he had gone to live in, nothing else. And that's when he told me about Seven Roads. And that's why I came."

Price's brow was still drawn in together.

"But why did he tell you at all? Why did he reach out after all of these years?"

"Because the old man was dying and I was the last stop on his attempt-at-redemption tour," she said.

"He felt guilty," Price guessed.

JJ shook her head. She laughed. It was unkind.

"No. He even told me he didn't regret what he did. What he *did* regret was what he believed would happen once he was gone."

"You mean after he died?"

JJ nodded.

"Apparently, word got around their organization that he had let evidence disappear that could destroy all of them. Then, after some digging, they found out that he'd not only let it go, but he'd let it go with a surprise survivor from the accident. Able Ortiz's flesh-and-blood child. The only problem was, they thought it was the wrong one."

"Your brother."

"My brother, someone I didn't even know existed until that moment."

"That's why Lawson is looking for him," Price realized. "He thinks your brother has access to this all-destroying evidence?"

She nodded.

"Jonathan said he was holding off any moves the best he could but, after he died, he knew his son would use finding and officially dealing with the evidence and our family as a way to vie for the new leader of the group, instead of Jonathan's right-hand man."

"He's going to use it as a power play."

JJ nodded again.

"Jonathan told me he couldn't outright stop his son because, at the end of the day, it was his son, but that he could give me a fighting chance to maybe save my brother." JJ opened her arms wide and motioned around them. "I thought I was faster than Lawson but, apparently, he's moving just as quick."

She could have stopped there. Price wouldn't know that she'd held back.

Yet, those bright eyes kept looking at her like she was as normal as she had been when he'd picked her up earlier that night.

And that meant something to her.

That meant a lot to her, actually.

So, JJ added one last thing to her life's worth of chaos.

"What Jonathan Cole and his son *don't* know is that Riker and I have our own secret about that night too."

Price's eyebrow rose again.

JJ bit the bullet.

"We never had Dad's evidence to take them down. We bluffed."

Chapter Fourteen

Sunlight came home two hours before Winnie did. Price had expected her, and unlocked the door minutes before she was coming through it.

She had never ever been a fan of spending the night at other people's houses. She'd have fun, sure, but as soon as she could get someone to take her, she was back to the house looking hungover despite not having a drop to drink.

Her friend Abagail had an early riser for a mother, so Price had expected her.

If his mind wasn't working through a case in the background, he would have smiled at the predictability.

He did smile at her, though, as she trudged into the kitchen and dropped her bag next to the breakfast bar. She settled on one of the stools and reached her hands out with a pout.

"If you make me an egg bowl right now, I promise I won't complain *as much* next time we have to rake the ungodly amount of leaves in the backyard."

Price snorted and stepped to the side of the stove.

He had just finished scrambling one of his famous egg bowls.

"Remember you said that."

Winnie dropped her head in defeat but didn't complain.

"I'll have no regrets as long as I can eat something in the next minute," she said. "I love Abagail, I really do, but her family doesn't believe in snacks. The last time I ate was yesterday at like six. Not to be dramatic, but I think I could eat even Corrie's cooking at this point."

Price grabbed her a bowl and started to fill it.

"Not to be dramatic, but I think I'd rather go hungry than chance Corrie's cooking," he said. "Remember when she tried to get the coffee shop to eat that weird turkey dinner thing she made for Thanksgiving?" He pretended to shiver. "I'll take no-snacks Abagail's house over that any day."

Winnie agreed and took the bowl with a low bow and several thanks.

Price returned the gesture with a laugh and then started on the second of three bowls he'd planned on making.

"Did you at least get some sleep?" he asked over his shoulder.

Winnie said she did around a mouthful of food.

"We watched a few movies and I fell asleep toward the end of the second one. She might not have snacks, but her bed is super comfy. It also helped that her little brother was staying over at his friend's house too. He wasn't around to annoy us like usual."

Price paused, spatula in midair for a moment.

Less than eight hours ago, Price had learned everything there was to know about JJ Shaw.

Lydia Ortiz.

She had gone from the quiet, unassuming part-timer trying her hand at a slower pace of life…to a woman living a double life, hell-bent on scorching the earth to find her little brother.

"So it was you who I fought in Josiah's house that morning," Price had asked once her story had finished.

JJ had looked apologetic at that.

"Josiah fit the description, age and circumstances to possibly be my brother. I was keeping an eye on him, trying to figure out how to go about finding proof that he was when I heard about his call to the department about the suspicious hole. I thought the department brushed him off and, when he rushed off to work, I decided to go head and check it out. That's when you showed up. To be fair, I tried to leave without fighting you. You were just, well, in the way."

She'd given him a little smile at that.

Price had remembered her moves then. Not only had she hurt him, she'd been faster than him too.

"After that, though, I decided to lie low," she'd added. "Then I found Josiah."

They assumed Lawson, for whatever reason, had one of his men come in after her. It had only been a coincidence that she had seen him walking through the field.

"You were casing Jamie Bell's house after you heard he was leaving town for a few months," Price had guessed next.

JJ had nodded.

"I'm assuming Lawson heard the same news I did and, well, we decided to act sooner rather than later."

It had made sense then. What she had been doing to the door.

"Let me guess. One of your sneaky skills is lock picking," he'd said.

JJ didn't even try to hide it.

She'd put three fingers in the air.

"Scouts honor I only use it for good, not bad."

After that, she had promised that her behind-the-scenes sleuthing hadn't included any other questionable activities.

She had also been adamant that no one else knew about her existence and she hoped to keep it that way.

"I'm only here to find my brother and then figure out a way to keep him out of all of this long enough to find Dad's evidence, or at least figure out a way to take Lawson and his group down permanently."

Price had fixed her then with a searching look.

"If you find him, he might not want to stay out of it," he'd pointed out.

At that, JJ's expression had hardened. Her words had been just as hard.

"I don't plan on telling him who I am."

"What do you mean? You're not going to tell your brother that you're, well, his sister?"

JJ had shaken her head.

"I'm dangerous to him, with or without Lawson out of the picture. Besides him, there's still people in the organization who hate my dad. If I can't keep my brother from being targeted, I might have to put myself in their sights instead. And if that happens, I can't have any link to him. No one can know that Able and Elle Ortiz had two children."

Price had been struck silent at that.

Now, scrambling eggs in his kitchen while his daughter sighed into her food, he still couldn't find the words.

Only anger.

Rage.

And it all went to Lawson Cole.

He had already proven to be a problem at the convention center.

Now, in Price's eyes, he was the only problem.

Price placed the newest batch of eggs into a bowl and started on the last one.

Winnie's voice cut through his thoughts, bringing him fully back into the present.

"I guess I'm not the only one who was really hungry. I don't think I've ever seen you put down two egg bowls before. I'm not sure it's the best idea. Doesn't the bacon give you heartburn? You're going to need some TUMS."

Price rolled his eyes and waved her off with his free hand.

"While your concern is truly touching, for your information *this* is for JJ."

"Oh, you're doing food delivery to her house now? Last night must have been fun."

Price heard the footsteps echoing from the hallway behind them. He turned as Winnie made a sound between a cough and a sputter.

"Is that JJ? She spent the night?"

Before Price could answer, the woman in question came into view.

She had her hands up in a defensive gesture.

"I did but don't get any ideas," she told Winnie. "It was a stressful night, and we came here to talk about it after and, well, apparently that stress sent me straight to sleep. On the couch."

She pointed in the direction of the living room.

JJ wasn't entirely lying. Night had turned to early morning as they talked, so JJ had asked if she could stay on the couch until they reached a more acceptable hour to be potentially seen going home by her neighbors. Price, knowing her neighbors, doubted they would be awake but on the off chance they were, he agreed avoiding that gossip would be nice.

That, and the simple fact that Price hadn't actually wanted JJ to leave.

Sure, she had stuck around to tell him her story but that didn't mean she would continue to stick with him to see the rest of it through.

He had already thought she would run into the night after they had first gotten to his house and he'd left her in the truck alone.

Would he have tried to stop her if she had?

Would he go after her and tell the department what was going on?

Would he *still* tell the department what was going on?

Price believed JJ's story. He believed in her without any hard evidence, he had already realized.

Yet, that didn't mean he wanted to let her out of his sight now.

She was a person of interest.

He just wasn't sure what to do about that next.

Price handed the egg bowl over to JJ. Winnie was doing her best to change her expression from shock to belief. Price had to admit, this was the first time in her years of living that he'd had a woman spend the night.

He gave her some room to collect herself and took his food to the breakfast bar too. JJ settled down on the last of the three stools on the other side of her.

If this had been the JJ of yesterday afternoon, he wondered if she would have played shy and apologetic on repeat. Instead, she seemed oddly at ease.

"Corrie would have loved the party," she said after a few bites of her food. "We schmoozed with a lot of people we didn't even need to, but your dad here was a talking machine. I don't think there was a person we met who escaped his conversation."

That made Winnie jump in surprise. She laughed.

"Deputy Little says that Dad is a bad guy's worst night-mare. He can just talk them into the ground if he needs to."

Price rolled his eyes.

"The goal of last night *was* talking," he reminded the ladies. "And, may I point out, Miss Shaw, that you never gave me a code word to help get you *out* of a conversation. So, I didn't see a reason to limit my abilities."

"Hey, I'm not upset at your chatter," JJ said. "It meant less work for me."

Price said he was glad to assist and, unlike the night before, Price simply listened as the two of them dove into small talk.

It was comfortable.

It made their small fight the night before feel like a dream.

"Lawson is clearly playing with fire—his man actually blew up half of a home—so don't you think we should too? With the department on your side, you'd have more fire-power yourself."

JJ's reaction had been immediate.

She'd been frowning so deeply that it seemed to pull her entire face down with it.

"The department has rules. Lawson has already shown that he isn't playing by any. I'm not going to either." That frown had managed to deepen somehow. "If you really want to help me, by association you're also breaking the rules. And, if something happens to my brother, or me, it could all come back to haunt you. So, you really need to think about wanting to help me before you agree to follow me into what might happen next."

JJ had told him to sleep on it. He'd followed her request and had.

It was simple math, really.

He was the law; JJ had been breaking it.

Lawson had done bad; JJ wanted vengeance.

An innocent man was being targeted; an innocent woman was gunning for the one doing the targeting.

Seven Roads was in danger; JJ Shaw had become a ghost to try and fight against it.

A brother was in trouble; his big sister had sacrificed herself to save him.

No matter which way Price ran the numbers, it had always come back to him feeling sympathy and anger.

He didn't have siblings, but he did have a daughter and there wasn't a part of him that wouldn't burn the entire world to save her. Thinking about JJ's parents having their children's futures taken from them was hard enough, but now to know that their nightmare hadn't ended? Now to know that their daughter was shouldering it all alone to try and end it for them?

Price wasn't sure which thought put more fire within him.

He'd told JJ the night before that he would think about it—really consider helping her while also keeping it a secret from everyone he knew—but the truth was, he hadn't considered it all.

Because Price had already decided the moment he'd seen Lawson Cole's hand around JJ's neck in that elevator.

She wasn't going to be alone ever again.

Not while he was around.

Chapter Fifteen

They dropped Winnie off for her shift at the coffee shop but didn't go in. They had other plans. Plans that included JJ letting Price into her home.

"It's pretty standard," she said after coming into the house from the garage. They had already shut his truck inside, hoping to keep his being there on the down-low. It wasn't in the middle of the night and not even early morning anymore, but still, JJ wanted to err on the side of discretion.

"The house, I mean," she tacked on. "It was already furnished when I bought it. I think most of this comes from a show house, to be honest. It's a very furniture storeroom floor kind of vibe. But it works."

JJ felt a flash of nerves at having the deputy in her personal space. Then again, she had just insisted that she sleep on his couch the night before. It didn't seem right to shoo him away from her house, especially since it wasn't exactly special.

There was only one room that held any kind of sentiment for her, and she still needed to hype herself up for that.

"I don't think it's standard," Price replied, politely. He motioned around the living room. "It's neat. Unlike my vibe of an explosion at a yard sale. You've seen how many little things I have collecting dust."

JJ remembered all the family and friends in pictures that he had framed and displayed.

She had only a handful and, of those, they had all been carefully curated to uphold her backstory if anyone ever visited. As for little knickknacks and collectibles, she had none. JJ had spent the better part of her life building skills, not hobbies. Fun memories? Those were few and far between.

It hadn't bothered her before. Yet now she couldn't help but feel self-conscious about it. Like they had just left a warm room filled with music and stepped into a cold expanse of silence.

Just to cut through it, she fumbled with the TV remote and turned the flat-screen TV on.

"Make yourself at home while I run and take a quick shower." She tossed him the remote. "I'll be back in a jiffy."

JJ hurried to her bedroom, threw together a fresh change of clothes and was in the shower before the water could even heat the rest of the way up.

Price Collins was in her home and not just for a visit. He was there to talk about her brother, Lawson Cole and how to deal with both. It made her feel jittery, but not necessarily in an uncomfortable way.

If JJ was being honest with herself, she was excited.

Not just to have someone to help, but to have Price's help.

He had surprised her, more than once, since meeting him. He seemed like a good, charming guy who was quick with a joke, easy for a smile. He was a great father, evident in how close he and Winnie were. A good friend too, based on the fact that even Corrie couldn't disparage the man.

But that wasn't the end of it.

JJ had seen it while she was in the elevator. She'd seen

it fighting with the man in the hood at Jamie Bell's. She'd seen it while fighting him herself at Josiah's.

Price had an edge to him.

A sharpness that could split.

It was the same sharpness she had seen when he had pulled her aside after breakfast.

"I'm in."

Two words.

Simple, but even as she showered, they made her stomach flutter.

"Pull yourself together," she told herself in between the shower's streams of water.

Lawson and his group weren't just a what-if anymore.

They were real and they were already here.

JJ didn't dillydally after that. She dressed in a pair of jeans and a simple tee, braided her wet hair and only applied light makeup. She had grown used to not putting perfume on, afraid that she would make herself *too* memorable while trying to stay beneath the radar, though she paused next to her jewelry box.

There were simple things in it. A few necklaces, rings and earrings that also weren't all that memorable. JJ picked up the only thing inside with color.

It was blue, square and had an almost-worn-away flower painted on its surface. Two smaller circle beads sat on top and beneath the square. It was a hanging earring, dangling the beads on a silver wire, clumsily knotted and glued at its end.

There was only one.

JJ was feeling nostalgic. She slipped it in her right ear and smiled.

Then she was down to business.

She wasn't the only one.

Price had his hands on his hips and was staring down at the dining room table when she found him. He wasn't in a suit, but his profile screamed that he was definitely a man who took a few trips to the gym. She remembered landing a hit against those same muscles at Josiah's. She wondered what he would feel like in a more ideal position.

A butterfly dislodged in her stomach.

That butterfly went back and grabbed a friend.

Price turned to her, brows drawn together and oblivious to the encroaching blush pushing up her neck.

"I'm guessing you're not the kind of person to write down important information you want to keep secret, huh?"

JJ tucked her chin a little and went around to stand opposite him. He had a piece of paper and pen on the table. It had three names on it: Josiah Teller, Jamie Bell and Marty Goldman.

She tapped her temple.

"I don't like leaving a trail, no," she said. "Riker used to joke that I would make a good super villain if I ever felt so inclined. I tend to do everything as analog or off-the-books as possible. Ironic, considering I'm going after a group who employs some of the same values."

Price waved a hand dismissively through the air between them.

"But you're using your powers for good, not evil, so I'll say it evens out." He pointed to the list of names. "Me? I need to see some ink to think. And, yes, I know that rhymed."

JJ held in a smile. Price's expression had gone sharp again.

He wasn't trying to be charming.

He was trying to work.

"Okay, so you found these guys through adoption records you may or may not have used your computer powers to get," he kept on. "You said there's two more names you found that fit the bill? The same age, adopted, and living in Seven Roads? I'm honestly surprised there's more than one with that description, let alone five."

JJ took the paper and pen and spun both around.

"Well, apparently, Marty Goldman didn't count," she reminded him. "As you were smart enough to throw out to Lawson—even though you had no idea what was going on, by the way—Marty's adoption was a lie. One his parents came up with after realizing his mother had an affair and then ended up working it out and staying together. His record of adoption was less a record and more a collection of posts I found mentioning it." She tapped Josiah and Jamie's names. "These are the only two I actually found official documents for, though I couldn't find the specifics like when they were adopted. That's why I needed to get into their homes to see their official paperwork. Or something that might convince me they were my brother."

She wrote down two more names.

"These last names are *mostly* based on hearsay and, I had been hoping, two names I wouldn't have to check in person yet."

Price leaned over.

She watched his eyes widen at one of them.

"Before you say it, I know," she said. "Connor Clark. He's going to be a problem."

Price shook his head. He tapped the other name.

"No, Anthony Boyd is going to be the problem. He needs to be the last person we look at, and really hope we don't have to. Connor Clark? He's actually doable."

"You know both?"

He shrugged.

"Connor is a high school teacher, or has been, for a few years now. He spoke at Winnie's freshmen orientation before she started school. And I *only* remember who he is so clearly because every single mom in there was drooling. He's a looker."

In the most casual way possible, Price brought his gaze up to hers. Then it roamed across her before he nodded.

"I guess you'd have that in common if he really is your brother."

Price's attention went right back to the paper.

JJ was glad for the break because every inch of her face felt like it was on fire.

"I don't know where he lives, but I do know it's somewhere near the school," he continued. "As for any family, adoptive or otherwise, I haven't heard anything. How did you end up flagging him?"

JJ cleared her throat as discretely as possible before she answered.

"Uh, there's an online fostering and adoption Facebook group for the state. He commented on a post where someone was asking advice on when they should tell their child that they had been adopted as a baby."

"What did he say?"

"'Being adopted isn't something that is embarrassing or should be kept hidden. Normalizing it as part of the child's story will only help them realize that it is normal.' Something to that effect at least. He also liked several comments that suggested they tell their child when they're old enough to understand and to mention it often."

"Which might not be enough to put him on your list but I'm assuming he's also the same age?"

JJ nodded.

"He also lived here when he was a kid before leaving for college."

"And how did you get Boyd on here?" Price asked. He didn't sound as enthused anymore.

"Anthony Boyd was adopted by his stepmother when he was a baby. I couldn't find any pictures of his biological mother on any searches I ran. I didn't want to rule him out as a possibility until I could find out if his father had any pictures of his mother around or talk to him about her. The problem is with that—"

"That Anthony Boyd's father passed when he was a teen, his stepmom remarried and moved, and currently he lives and works on my least favorite place in Seven Roads. The Becker Farm, run by the meanest and nosiest old man I ever met."

JJ felt her eyebrow go up.

"Price Collins has someone he doesn't like that much?" she had to ask.

Price grumbled.

"More like Becker doesn't like me. You get caught *once* fooling around in his barn in high school and he holds a grudge like a hamster holds food in his cheeks." He sobered. "Have you asked Corrie about these guys? She's a gossip magnet. Even if she doesn't know the backstory herself, she could probably get it for you."

JJ had already considered that avenue, but the fact of the matter was, she'd already used it three times.

"I learned a lot from her about the first three names on the list. I don't want to push my luck. Or hers." Now that Lawson was around, she didn't need him hearing about a woman asking after two names he might or might not have already.

Price seemed to pick up on that thought.

"So what's the plan, then?" he asked after a moment. "What do you want to do?"

She believed that Price had accepted her story, but JJ was on edge about her next steps.

Price was the law. Would he really help her break it if she needed to?

JJ cleared her throat. This time it wasn't because he'd made her blush.

"We try to talk to them to see if we can figure out where they came from."

Price must have picked up on her change in worries.

His bright eyes raised to hers.

"And if talking doesn't work?" he asked.

JJ kept her voice just as strong.

"Then we improvise."

Lawson slammed his fist on the tabletop. He was frustrated; he was energized.

"There's one last name we could think of that might have a tie to the Ortiz child," the man across from his said. "I have someone going out there to check on it. But—"

"But that deputy just went with that woman of his to the farm," he finished, rehashing the information he had just been given himself.

The man nodded.

"I don't know how much Deputy Collins knows about what we're doing, but since he's been at the last three scenes, I don't think it's too much of a stretch to say he's tangled up with us."

Lawson hit the tabletop again. Now he was just frustrated.

"Dad said he made a deal with Ortiz's partner all those years ago to keep it a secret. Who's to say they didn't loop in any more law enforcement? Or maybe the son himself could have if he realized who his dad was." He clenched his fist. "This. This is why my father was a fool. We have no idea what to expect with this supposed evidence floating around out there. That's why we need to destroy it once and for all. And anyone who's even remotely related to it."

The man nodded.

Lawson grumbled.

"What about the deputy's woman?" he asked after a moment. "Can we use her?"

"Normal. Southern polite, works at the coffee shop in town alongside the deputy's daughter. I'm guessing that's how they met."

Lawson sat up straight.

"Wait. Did you say that Deputy Collins has a daughter?"

"Yep. Seventeen-year-old girl."

Lawson's mind starting spinning. He smiled after a moment.

"Does she go to the high school?"

The man nodded again.

Lawson's smile turned into a smirk.

He was back to energized.

"Send someone to this farm and keep an eye on the deputy and his awful woman."

The man tilted his head in question.

"What about our lead? The teacher?"

Lawson was nothing but smug now.

"I think we might have just found a way to kill a lot of birds with only one, very effective stone."

Chapter Sixteen

Improvising came quicker than either of them expected.

"When I offered to help, this wasn't what I thought you meant."

Price was ducked down, one shoulder tucked against a wall, the other facing an open field. JJ was in front of him in the same stance. Instead of turning to address him, though, she swung her hand back. It wasn't a slap, but it hit her mark.

Her hand covered his mouth.

"You wanted to be here so hush."

The sudden contact threw him off, but he still smiled against her palm. The sweet image of JJ Shaw had been one he'd already found interesting. Once the act had dropped? Well, he was finding this JJ to be entirely entertaining.

Even when she had them doing something that wasn't exactly on the up-and-up.

JJ dropped her hand and used it to point ahead of them.

"Your friend said Boyd lived in the barn, right? That's the new one?"

By his friend, she was referring to the son of the owner of Becker Farm. Instead of willy-nilly breaking and entering, he had tried to use casual conversation to get information on Anthony Boyd's whereabouts. It had made for a slightly awkward conversation in the beginning, but Price had saved it by an excuse of potentially needing help with future home renovations. Anthony Boyd's strength was well known, considering that had been one of the main reasons a grump like Old Man Becker had hired someone not from his bloodline.

"He's not in town, though," the junior Becker had told Price over the phone. "He and Dad are in Alabama for a livestock auction. They won't be back until Monday. Want me to get Boyd to call you then?"

Price had thanked him for the offer and said he'd reach out again himself.

That had green-lit JJ Shaw, who was currently sneaking her way across the back of one of the storage buildings on the Becker Farm.

"If no one's home, this might be the easiest and quickest way we have to look at what we need," JJ had said, coaxing him outside of the western gate of the farm. "If it's not Boyd? Then no one will ever know we were looking for anything. No one gets suspicious and no one's in potential danger. It's a win-win."

Now she waved an impatient hand back at him.

"He said new barn, right?" she repeated. "Is that the one right up there?"

Price hadn't seen the new barn in person, but he definitely knew where the old one was. He nodded and pointed.

"We should see it once we turn the corner."

True enough, the moment they rounded the storage building they had a straight sight line to a structure that Price hadn't seen before. It was all traditional on the outside—red and white, stall doors tall and wide, and all types of tools and equipment parked on the dirt patch outside—but the junior Becker had taken the time to talk about how it was unlike any of the buildings on the farm.

He'd been proud to say that he had approved Boyd's living quarters, located as an apartment on the second floor.

"I'm assuming those stairs lead right up to the apartment." Price pointed to the stairs on the outside of the barn. JJ bobbed her head this way and that for a moment.

"I don't see any security cameras mounted anywhere." Price snorted.

"And you won't find any on the property," he said. "Old Man Becker likes his privacy. Even from himself. He'd sooner do rounds every hour on the hour than let electronics and the internet do it for him."

JJ nodded and didn't talk after that. She led the way across the open land with surprising speed. Though, maybe it wasn't that surprising to Price anymore. She *had* been the one in the mask who had managed to outrun him at Josiah's.

The same person he had fought.

The same person who he'd managed to hit pretty decently.

Then, a few hours later, he had been helping her with her car like nothing had happened.

Price mentally paused.

A new thought occurred to him, but he kept it quiet for the moment.

They took the stairs careful but quick. JJ already had her handy-dandy bag opened and her lock-picking tools out. Price snaked a hand past her and tried the doorknob first.

It turned with ease.

"I thought you said he wasn't home," JJ whispered in a rush.

Price opened the door.

"He's not, but I'd bet living on this land gives you a false sense of security," he said. "Because who would be reckless enough to tempt fate when it comes to ticking off the Becker patriarch?"

He went past her and into the dark space. When he flicked the light switch on, he was already impressed.

The apartment above the barn was indeed an apartment. Small, but nice. There was a full kitchen that opened into the living room and a small nook beside it that housed a desk and chair for a workspace. Two doors were open at the back wall, showing the bedroom and the bathroom, respectfully.

No one jumped out and yelled at their intrusion.

Nothing but them moved at all.

"This is nice," Price had to comment aloud. "Good for Boyd."

JJ lightly pushed him deeper into the room so she could turn and shut the door behind them. He heard the deadbolt slide across behind him.

"Go ahead and take it in so we can start taking it apart," she said. "Let's see if we can find where he keeps his important documents first."

Price wasn't a fan of going through someone else's private things, but he had to admit that JJ's method of searching was...different than what he had expected.

She was like a surgeon, but a surgeon who didn't know which type of surgery they would be performing yet. There was a precision to her, a methodology she was adhering to that was clearly in her head. Her eyes were sharp, her gloved fingers nimble. She was taking in the details but at the same time, it felt like she was discarding them the second she realized they were of no use to her.

It still wasn't right what they were doing, but of the *not* rightness it wasn't bad.

Or you're only okay with it because she's JJ.

The thought pushed itself to the top of his mind in a flash.

It caught him off guard enough to physically wave his hand through the air like he was clearing it out.

JJ caught the motion.

"What's wrong?" she asked.

Price sidestepped a real answer and got to the other thought he'd pushed aside earlier.

"So you were doing this when I came to Josiah's, right?"

"I was actually on my second round, worried I missed something," she said with a nod. "I would have tried to restrain you to do it but thought better of it since I'd already done a thorough search. Plus, you ended up being a pain."

There was a hint of humor in her voice.

"A pain who showed up on your doorstep a few hours later." Price eyed a collection of books near them. None looked to fit the bill of what they were looking for. "Which, now that I think about it, I'm realizing your car breaking down was probably an excuse you told Corrie to get out of working."

He saw the corner of her lips turn up. She put the papers she had been looking through back on the desktop.

"Let's go see if there's a safe or something similar in the bedroom," she suggested.

Price put his head back and chuckled.

"Wow," he breathed out. "How did I not notice it was you? And here I thought I was observant."

"To be fair, I don't think most people would have thought it was me behind the mask. I also put on heels."

He followed her into the bedroom.

"Heels?"

She nodded.

"When I realized who you were when you came to my house, I put on heels so I was taller than when we fought. I was worried too many similarities might really push my luck."

Price remembered her sandals and their wedged height when he'd first officially met her that day. They had looked nice with her dress.

Turns out they were specifically to keep his suspicions at bay.

Price shook his head.

"You sure are something, Miss Shaw."

She was already at the side of the bed, opening the nightstand.

"I'll take that as a compliment, Deputy Collins."

They spent the next few minutes searching in silence. Anthony Boyd didn't have a safe or any kind of area that had a collection of seemingly important things. He was a spartan guy, all things considered. The pictures he had displayed were no exception.

"He put up all of the typical events," JJ observed. "Graduation, birthdays and a few candids of who looked like friends. Have you seen any pictures of his dad, though?"

Price tapped one on the dresser next to the bed.

"Here. It's the only one though."

JJ sidled up to him. She peered down at the picture.

"He might just not be good at pictures," Price noted. "Just because he doesn't have a lot with his parents, doesn't necessarily mean there's anything there."

JJ sighed.

Price thought back to her home from earlier that morning.

Maybe *home* wasn't the right word. It was a house. A place where she slept and ate but living? It had reaffirmed the description that he'd come up with for the woman already.

Ghost.

She was going through the motions of living while trying to stay detached from the very same people.

What if she did find her brother? What if she did take down Lawson and his group?

Would she really not tell her brother who she was?

Would she just disappear from his life?

From Seven Roads?

From Price?

Her hand startled his thoughts. The fabric of her gloves curled into his palm.

If her expression hadn't changed so drastically, Price might have mistaken the move as something else. Instead, she was facing the open door, tense.

"Did you hear that?"

No sooner than she asked, he heard the front door rattling.

He shared a quick look with JJ. Her eyes were wide.

Someone was coming in.

THEY JUST TRIED the doorknob. When the door didn't give, the movement stopped. Price didn't. He took JJ by the waist, she assumed to shuttle them into the closet or under the bed to hide next, but then stayed himself.

His hand rested on her hip while his gaze was glued to the door.

She wasn't doing anything differently.

JJ watched as the doorknob shook a few more times then went still.

There were only three options now: unlock the door, break the lock to open the door or walk away.

She knew which option she preferred. It was one thing for her to be caught in Anthony Boyd's apartment. It was an entirely different matter for a deputy of the law to be caught. That was without all the messy questions of why they were together too.

Maybe she could distract whoever came in while Price hid.

Maybe they both could hide.

Maybe—

"They're walking back down the stairs." Price's voice was low.

JJ strained to listen.

It was faint but he was right. She could hear retreating footfalls against the wooden stairs outside.

"Why would they leave?" she asked, more to herself than him.

They shared a look.

Then they were moving in tandem to the only window that lined the left wall. JJ was nimble in moving the simple curtain over the kitchen sink just enough to get a view of the side yard below. She couldn't see the end of the stairs, but the two men were easy targets as they walked across toward the front of the barn.

Adrenaline shot through JJ faster than lighting to a rod deep in a storm cloud.

She couldn't get a good view of the face of the shorter man, but the one in dark joggers and tennis shoes had a face she wouldn't forget.

"He's the one we fought at Jamie Bell's," she said, voice pitching higher than she meant to. "Why are they here? Are they following us?"

Price's expression went razor-sharp.

"Let's find out."

Chapter Seventeen

JJ didn't like regrets. But, well, she was big enough to admit that she had a few.

Pain seared up her leg, her elbow throbbed and something felt like it was in her eye. The only thing that didn't have any complaints on her happened to be her head. Which was nice, considering she'd had a concussion not that long ago.

Did she regret her almost year-long journey to trying to quietly and calmly find her brother? No.

Did she regret breaking the law, fighting off bad guys and going up against Lawson by herself? No.

Did she regret sharing her life story and current plan with Price Collins, charming deputy with an easy smile and warm hands? Not at all.

Did she slightly, a little, maybe kind of regret not listening to him back at the barn and chasing one of the men all the way into the woods while he dealt with the other, only to fall down a rather steep hill, making herself an easy target for said man? Well, she couldn't say she *didn't* regret it.

She didn't recognize this man, but made the assumption that he might have been the one who had attacked Josiah Teller after she had left his house.

And that jump in conclusion happened all thanks to the

knife he had in his hand as he backtracked to the spot at the bottom of the hill where she was currently struggling.

All the training and skills she had accumulated through the years took a back seat while she scrambled to pull air back into her lungs. The impact of the fall had done more than a number on her.

"Your hands go into your pockets at all, and I cut them off." The man's voice came out strong and full of oxygen. He was a few yards away but closing that distance fast.

JJ put her hands up in defense. Her leg muscles worked double-time to push her to stand.

"Un-unarmed," she managed to say.

The man kept coming.

JJ hadn't seen the state of Josiah's house after his attack, but she had seen the man. The cuts, the blood... She could fight against a knife but, the truth was, knives scared her simply for the fact that she could imagine what a cut felt like. The pain and sting. It was all too easy to imagine what the man could do without having it actually happen.

"Stop—stop," she said around a cough.

He still didn't.

So JJ took a lesson out of her godfather's page of parenting.

"Chicken—chicken wings!"

Her voice had found some more of its strength. The man she'd just yelled at heard what she said loud and clear.

And it made him slow.

"What?" he asked.

JJ took a tentative step backward.

If she hadn't fallen, she could have cut off his attempt to pull his knife out. Now? She needed help. Preferably her partner with the gun. JJ, at least, assumed Price had his service weapon on him.

Either way, two people against one very sharp-looking knife sure sounded more strategic than one.

"Spaghetti!" JJ yelled, this time louder than before. "Fruit Roll-Ups, hummus, Pringles!"

The man's eyebrow rose but the rest of him paused.

She had confused him enough to have him stop in his tracks.

The second he stalled, she went into gear.

JJ spun around and ran along the bottom of the hill, hoping for an easier way up than the tumultuous path she had taken down. The man cussed behind her. She wasn't going to be a damsel from a movie and look back. Instead, she tucked her chin and made fast work of searching out more even ground. She couldn't have been that far away from Price. Once she was at the top of the slope, she could probably see where he was detaining the man from Jamie Bell's house.

"Winnie Collins!"

JJ came to an almost instant halt.

She whirled around, utterly confused.

The man with the knife also stopped but he kept his knife pointed out at her.

"See? I can yell stuff too." He moved the aim of his knife to a spot in the distance. "But I'm guessing you don't have spaghetti or chicken tied up in your car, do you? That's where our things are different."

JJ's stomach dropped past her feet.

Maybe she hadn't heard him properly?

"Who?"

The man looked fragile by himself. There were wrinkles along his face, a scar at the side of his jaw, and a slight lean to him, like he had an injury somewhere along his leg or back?

Had Josiah managed to wound him during their fight?

The knife, however, was the line in the sand between them.

That was, until he said Winnie's name.

He said it again too.

"Winnie Collins. Your boyfriend's little girl." He smirked. "What? You think we were following you just for fun? I'm here to trade. I can do that with you while my friend deals with dear Dad Deputy."

The knife didn't seem so bad anymore.

It was maybe five inches long, some of that the metal hilt. The blade wasn't serrated and didn't retract. If she could stay on the back of it, she could handle it.

"She's in your car? Where's that? We didn't see any cars when we came in."

The man's smirk was simmering. He thought he had her.

"We hid ours with yours, of course. Since you two seem to be so good at being so sneaky. Too bad the girl didn't have your stealth."

Price's truck was at the western gate of the Becker Farm. The walk to the barn had been around two minutes. They hadn't gone into the woods but instead skirted them, careful to stay somewhat within the tree line.

JJ pointed in the direction he had.

"You want to trade me for Winnie?" she asked.

He nodded.

"Why?"

Did they know who she was, or had she become a pawn to use against Price?

The man's smirk melted away at that.

He was impatient.

It probably didn't help that his friend hadn't rejoined

him. The last they had seen of their partners had been Price wrestling cuffs on the other man.

"We'll talk at the car," he growled. "Get going or you and the girl will be sorry."

JJ didn't weigh her options. She knew what she needed to do.

She nodded and started in the direction of the western gate. She kept her hands up. The man didn't hesitate. She could hear his shoes crunching over the leaves behind her.

Then he changed the game yet again.

"You sure acted better than that girl when we grabbed her," he added. "She was still blubbering when we left."

JJ stumbled. It slowed her down two steps. The man moved diagonally just behind her.

"She cried that much?" JJ ventured.

The man snorted.

"Buckets. But I guess most girls would lose it when they know they're in danger. Why? You can't believe your kid doesn't have the stones to not make a peep?"

That cinched it.

"No," she said. "She just doesn't seem the type."

THE MAN HAD some moves, Price would give him that. He got his cuffs out and on one wrist before the man was a snake in the grass. He slithered this way and that until Price lost his grip.

The second the man realized he was free, he was off and running.

It surprised Price. He thought the man he'd fought in Jamie Bell's house would have more, well, fight in him. Especially without the threat of fighting against the speed of a fire. But the man turned into a rabbit and made quick time of leaving the land next to the barn and running right along the tree line like it was nothing.

Part of Price wanted to change direction and chase after JJ and the other man. The other part wanted to keep up with his suspect *for* JJ. He was a part of her family's trouble. Which meant he could help lead them to a way to solve it.

He couldn't let that lead go.

Not when he was this close.

I'm actually really good at fighting.

JJ's words from the elevator echoed in his head as he made the final decision to track his guy. Then it was an all-out race.

Price put everything he had into each step. His lungs burned. His muscles complained. The service weapon in its holster at his hip beneath his jacket bumped along for the ride. He wasn't going to pull it out.

Not yet.

Not when all he had to do was—

They were moving along the curve of the tree line when the open land between the woods and the western gate came into view.

Instead of a big nothing, Price nearly lost his footing when he saw a whole someone trucking it in the same direction as the gate.

It was a woman.

"JJ?" he yelled out, voice strong despite his running.

Thankfully, it carried.

He could see her head turn their way.

But she didn't stop.

If anything, she picked up speed toward the gate.

It was unsettling.

It also was distracting.

The man he was chasing had slowed.

It cost him the lead.

Price grabbed hold of the back of his jacket and pulled him to stop. They were both going too fast. The move threw off their respective balances and they hit the ground. Price was ready for it though. The man was not.

He yelled out as the ground was unkind to him.

Pain pulsed into Price's knees and palms, but he was in control right after.

He took the cuffs still attached to the man's wrist and finished the job.

"Don't—don't move," Price said through clenched teeth.

The man didn't try. He was making a noise between a whimper and a groan. Price didn't wait to see if he was hurt or not. He was staring into the distance.

JJ had made it to the gate, but he couldn't see what she was doing.

Then she switched direction and was coming back at him.

Like a moth drawn to a flame, Price's feet had him running toward her before he even realized what he was doing.

That run became feral as he realized two things.

One, JJ wasn't just running. She was running and holding herself. He couldn't see where it was coming from, but blood stained her shirt. And not just a little.

Two, she was yelling something, and it was a desperate yell. Fear seemed to be seeping from her face right into her words.

And, when she was close enough, that fear went from her and exploded within him.

"Call Winnie!" she yelled.

Price collided with JJ, stopping them both. JJ kept yelling despite being tucked into his chest.

"Call Winnie now!"

All the blood in Price's body seemed to freeze. He didn't question her. It didn't feel like there was time. He pulled his cell phone out of his pocket and fumbled to unlock it. He had Winnie's caller ID up and the call started within the space of a terrified heartbeat.

JJ angled herself against him, so her face was pressed against his, phone between both of their ears. Her breathing was ragged. Price would later realize his was too. In that moment though, every fiber of his being was agonizing through a ringback tone that seemed to last forever.

However, it only really lasted two rings.

"Hey, Dad." Winnie's voice came through loud and clear.

"Are you okay?" he asked.

"I'm bored at work but yeah. Why?"

JJ deflated against him. Price had to reinforce his hold around her. She kept her face against his and spoke into the phone before he could respond.

"Winnie, go give your phone to Corrie," she rasped out. "I—I need to talk to her."

JJ reached up and took the phone as Winnie said an unsure okay. She pushed off Price and dug into the bag she had been wearing across her chest. It was covered in blood. She unzipped it and took her own cell phone out. She handed it over.

Corrie answered the phone before she could explain.

"Corrie? This is JJ. I need you to close the coffee shop and drive Winnie to the sheriff's department. Right now. Don't stop for anyone or anything. Got me?"

Price had never heard JJ sound so cold.

She met his eye.

"I'll stay on the line with you until you get there."

Price understood her phone now.

She wanted him to call the department.

Something bad must have happened. Something more than the blood on her.

Not only had he never heard her sound so cold, Price hadn't seen JJ look so scared.

He nodded.

Then he called the sheriff directly.

Liam answered quickly.

Price didn't waste either of their time.

"I need two cars and an ambulance over at the Becker Farm. But, Sheriff, I need you to stay at the department. I'm sending my daughter your way."

Price shared another long look with JJ.

He didn't know what was going on but, in that moment, he trusted no one more than the woman who had been leading a double life.

Chapter Eighteen

The world had a funny way of still turning, no matter what JJ was feeling.

She could be confused, happy, healthy, bleeding, disgusted, enraged, missing her mama, craving ice cream, thinking about that one smell of disinfectant that only ever seemed to exist in the hospital hallway...

She could be in a plane, on a couch, wearing a fancy dress or hanging upside down in car drenched in rain with a sea of glass beneath her hair...

And it just didn't seem to matter to the world at large.

It kept turning. It kept going.

It kept leaving JJ in its dust to figure it all out so she could catch up before the next swing got her.

She was standing behind a two-way glass, staring into an interrogation room and looking at a man handcuffed to the table. His world had him angry, frustrated, defiant. All three were written on his face and spelled out clear in how he fought everyone tooth and nail since he'd been arrested.

"He wouldn't give us a name and we can't find him in any database." Sheriff Weaver's badge was shining on his belt. He seemed to be handling his world in stride. Ever since the call with Price, he hadn't taken a step he didn't want to take. Not even when it had come to Price explaining that they couldn't give answers to everything just yet.

That *just yet* wasn't going to extend that much further, though, if JJ had to guess.

Especially since she was about to show the man in charge that she wasn't just some bystander.

Instead of being helpless at the window, JJ sighed.

"I think we need to talk now, if you don't mind."

A few minutes later and JJ's world brought her to a small room with a big table. The sheriff sat in a chair at its side, Price stood near its head and JJ felt lost in between. Her arm hurt, her leg was already bruising, and everything she had worked for felt like it had already crumbled.

The best she could do now was hope to be standing again when the next swing around came for her.

JJ started by tapping her cell phone on the top of the table.

"I can find out who that man is, most likely, but I need to ask for something first." She started in the last place she meant to. Bartering with the head of the law when she was in no position to do so.

Sheriff Weaver, to his credit, didn't immediately shut her down.

"I would really appreciate if we could not connect me with any of what's happened," she continued. "Any mention of my name in reports or posts or interviews. I'm not saying make it where Price was alone during everything, but just don't put JJ Shaw in any kind of writing. Ideally, call in the people who saw me today and ask them to keep my name out of their mouths too."

Sheriff Weaver tilted his head a little. He'd been rumored to be a quiet, loner of a man until he had met his now-wife, just as he was also rumored to be a no-nonsense man when it came to his job. JJ could see that no-nonsense man coming through now. He spoke right to the point.

"My people don't talk idly. I don't either. That said, I don't think a person in this town could promise that your name won't come up one way or the other."

JJ sighed again.

"But we can slow talk down, at least," she said. "It could give me time to…adjust."

Price took a step closer to JJ so that he was facing the sheriff more directly at her side.

"I've already talked to everyone who saw her. They said they won't say anything."

JJ cast a quick look at Price.

How long had they been separated that he had that time?

He had been with her when the EMT had bandaged her arm. He had been with her when Detective Williams and Deputy Little had shown up. He had been with her when they had found the man she'd fought.

When had he left her side?

She had seen how tightly he'd hugged Winnie when they made it to the department. How all of him had dragged down in relief that she was really okay.

Was she missing time in between?

JJ didn't ask. The sheriff looked between them. She couldn't read his expression.

Was she even trying to?

JJ's phone sat on the table between them.

She didn't want to use it; she knew she would.

"I know someone who might be able to find out who that man is," she went on. "But before I do, I have to warn you that he's a source I need to protect. I would *like* for my name to stay out of all of this, but I *need* his to stay absolutely clear of it. Will that be okay?"

She added the last part to feel more polite but, the truth was, even she heard the lack of wiggle room in what she phrased as a request.

Sheriff Weaver didn't kick up a fuss.

"I'll respect your terms as long as it doesn't run the risk of harming anyone. Yourself included."

That wasn't a quick no.

That wasn't a permanent yes.

JJ had little room to ask for more.

"Let me make the call and then I'll tell you everything," she added. "I'll be right back."

The sheriff okayed the move. JJ wasn't sure what she would have done had he not. She felt like the world definitely wasn't slowing down as her feet led her to the only room in the department that she thought would keep her shielded from the growing anxiety in her chest.

The ladies' room had two stalls inside, and both were empty. JJ felt a tinge of disappointment. She didn't have to pretend to be okay for a little longer. She didn't have to play her role as calm and mysterious.

She didn't have to pretend that she wasn't spiraling.

Instead, she was faced with her reflection.

The bandage along her arm was long. She had been lucky to only get the long cut. Lucky that it hadn't needed stitches. Her shirt was ruined, stained beyond saving, but it was her phone that pulled at her attention like a beacon in the darkness.

She went to her contacts, but couldn't go past the first name on the list.

Dad.

A wallop of anguish slammed into JJ's chest. She didn't want to see herself anymore. She grabbed the sink with one hand and clutched the phone to her chest with the other as she moved out of the mirror's scope. Her back hit the tiled wall between the sink and the wall with a painful thud. She closed her eyes as a lump formed in her throat.

She smelled her strawberry shampoo.

The sound of the door opening made her open her eyes.

JJ could feel the part of her used to putting on a mask try its hardest to bring up a polite smile and a reasonable excuse for why she was all but crying in the corner of the bathroom, covered in blood and clutching her phone.

But then she saw who had come inside.

She watched as Price turned around, shut the door and locked it.

She watched as he walked slowly to the spot in front of her.

She watched as he fixed her with a look that was as quiet as velvet.

Then he took her face in his hands.

"Thank you." His words were soft but genuine. That confused her even more.

"For what?" she asked.

Price ran one hand down so his index finger and thumb could hold her chin.

"You've spent so much time trying to stay out of the spotlight as much as possible but, today, you didn't hesitate to put yourself in the middle of it. For Winnie." He sighed. A small smile turned up the corner of his lips. "That was a mighty move, Miss Shaw."

JJ expected another thank you. Instead, she got something else entirely.

Price pressed his lips against hers in a kiss that was gentle. Quiet. Velvet.

It was only when he broke it that JJ realized she had broken first.

All the stress of the last few hours, the last few days, the last few years, pushed JJ down into Price's chest. She was crying soon after.

Price was simple with his actions as he was with his kiss.

He wrapped his arms around her and didn't say a word.

"I'D SAY WHAT you did was make some dang questionable choices but, I guess, at the end of the day I might have done the same."

The sheriff ran a hand down his face. They were in his office, but neither was sitting down. Liam was leaning against the corner of his desk and Price was leaning against the wall. Both had their bodies tilted toward the door. They didn't want to be overheard and had already buttoned up once when Winnie had come in asking for money for the vending machines.

Now they were alone again to circle the same drain they had been circling the last half hour.

"I would have looped you in had I thought it would do more good than harm," Price admitted. "I thought we still had time."

It was a sticky situation, no matter who had done the sticking. After JJ had made the call to her source, she had sat down and told her story to Liam while Price sat at her side. Her telling the sheriff had been a different experience from when she had told him. She'd been completely detached. Maybe because she was tired. Maybe because she was hurt. Either way, it came out as if being read off a teleprompter by a newscaster finishing off a twelve-hour shift.

It had been a far cry from the woman he had held in his arms in the bathroom.

"Up until now, there's been nothing to grab on to either," Price pointed out. "We were already looking for Josiah's and Georgie's attackers. All I got a day before you was the backstory."

Sheriff Weaver actually snorted.

"I have a feeling you have a few more details than me. Miss Shaw in there might have given me her story, but don't think I didn't notice the few nudges you sent her way."

He wasn't wrong.

When JJ had been about to mention her break-in and subsequent fight with Price at Josiah Teller's, Price had put pressure against her. He trusted the sheriff and knew he was a lot more lenient when it came to going off the books in certain situations but, in that moment, Price had found himself oddly protective.

JJ had gotten the hint and left the search out as well as her intention to conduct one at Jamie Bell's house. Instead, she had simply stated her findings as definitive "They aren't my brother" statements for each.

Marty Goldman's adventure had been a bit different.

Just as Lawson Cole's name and attack had changed the game for the sheriff while Winnie's mention had changed the players.

What Price had told JJ in the bathroom had been true. He recognized what she had done, even if the others didn't. When the man in the woods had lied about having Winnie, he had unknowingly forced JJ to pick her anonymity or the immediate action of making sure his daughter had been, and would continue to be, okay.

Price hadn't been in those woods. He hadn't seen her have to decide, but the best he could guess was that she had made the decision in record time.

Not only that, she had gone up against an armed man with nothing more than her hands to try and get to Winnie as fast as possible.

JJ Shaw had already sacrificed a normal life to try and save a man in secret. Now, she had sacrificed her identity at just the possibility that his daughter was in danger.

The least Price could do was protect as much of that identity as possible, even if that meant withholding from his friend, his boss and his colleagues.

JJ Shaw had told the truth to help him.

Lying to protect her?

Price had decided that was the least he could do.

Now he fixed his friend with an apologetic smile but didn't tell him he was wrong.

Sheriff Weaver, to his surprise, returned his own smile.

"I know it might be a strange thing to say, but sometimes you remind me of my wife," he said.

Price placed a hand to his chest.

"Considering your wife's nickname is Sheriff Trouble, and she's one of the most epic people I've ever met? I'm honored."

The sheriff rolled his eyes.

"While she is those things, I meant the whole calculations thing." Liam tapped his head. "You're talking to me, but your numbers are running all around the people you're trying to keep safe. I'm even guessing you already have a plan to try and do that, with or without any of our help."

He wasn't wrong.

Since he had seen that Winnie was alright, Price had already started putting together a list of what happened next. Some of the items on that list had been dependent on how the sheriff would react to their news.

And how Lawson Cole would react to two of his lackeys being in custody.

"My main priority is making sure that Knife Guy's bluff of having Winnie doesn't ever become a reality," he pointed out. "If we can do that while running down Lawson Cole and his group while keeping JJ and her brother out of harm's way, I'd be counting my blessings every day for the rest of my life."

The sheriff nodded. Any teasing friendship disappeared. He was nothing but the sheriff when he spoke again.

"We'll hope that JJ's source comes through and can tell us who our man in custody is. Ideally, they'll know who the guy she sent to the hospital is too. Though, we won't be able to see him for a good while. Last I heard he might not make it."

They hadn't talked about it yet, but the fact was that JJ hadn't just fought against the man in the woods. She'd nearly killed him. Though he had gotten his licks in on her before she had gotten the upper hand. Price had spent the better part of an hour trying to convince her to go to the hospital. The only reason he hadn't been more forceful about it was thanks to the EMT who had taken a good look at the cut before bandaging it.

"As for Anthony Boyd and Connor Clark, I'm reading Darius in on the bare-bone facts when he gets back," Liam continued. "Between the two of us, we can try to figure out where they came from."

This was a point of contention.

The urge to protect JJ flared again.

The sheriff must have sensed it. He held up his hand in a stop motion.

"Your lady isn't the only one who can be clever when she wants to be," he added. "We'll keep everything low profile as well as keeping JJ's name away from all of this. Trust me."

The tension in Price's shoulders lessened but only minimally.

Liam's seemed to tighten.

His voice came out with undeniable command.

"Don't think though for one moment I'm letting you continue running around this town playing detective without a badge for it," he said. "It's time for you to leave. As of right now, Price Collins, you are officially benched."

Chapter Nineteen

Price stood shoulder to shoulder with Winnie. Each had a bag at their sides. Both were staring at the house behind JJ with grade A poker faces.

"I know it doesn't look like much, but the inside isn't as bad as, well, this." She motioned back to the work-in-progress two-story that she had purchased before coming to Seven Roads.

"It's…charming," Winnie tried, smiling as she did so. "Right? Kind of like one of those nice older homes you see on HGTV that everyone ends up wanting."

She not so subtly elbowed her dad's side when he didn't immediately respond.

Price took the hint. With his duffel bag held up by his hand over his shoulder and wearing his baseball shirt and jeans, he reminded JJ of a college student coming home after a long week at school. Young, carefree and ready to eat.

It wasn't a bad look.

In fact, it was almost nice to feel like he wasn't the same man who kept having to change his life around to deal with her problems.

Even now, he brought out that charm that JJ had begun to crave.

This time, it came out with some teasing.

"You definitely can't buy character like this much anymore." He grinned. "That's for sure."

"*Dad*," Winnie scolded in a not-so-quiet whisper. She sent another elbow to his ribs. He laughed and looked at JJ.

"As a former part-time home renovator, I understand that burden of the *before*. I ended up selling my fixer-upper to the sheriff's mother-in-law and haven't looked back." His words softened. "Don't stress about us. We're fine."

JJ wasn't so sure about that.

She said as much while leading them to the front porch.

"Let's remember you said that."

The old home off Whatley Bend was the center of JJ's cover story. She had purchased it as the reason for coming to Seven Roads, as well as the blueprint for her future. It had been chattered about in the gossip mill for a while when she had first come to town, but when no progress had been visibly made, that chatter had died down. It helped that Janice Wilkins's former home was less than accessible and not near any locations or public areas remotely interesting.

If anything, it felt like an outsider to JJ.

A part of the town but not, at the same time.

Maybe that's why she liked it, despite never having had any experience or desire to buy and renovate a house.

JJ bypassed the urge to explain why the siding was warped in places, wood was rotted off others and the landscaping could use a few—if not several—helping hands, and led them into the foyer. Winnie slipped off her shoes, but Price kept his and the duffel bag on. He had work to do, but he stayed long enough to listen to the two-bit tour.

"Everything in here works, but just isn't that nice-looking yet," she said, sweeping her arms toward the stairs just off the space. "This goes to two bedrooms, one bonus room that looks like a wasteland where supplies and tools have gone to die, and two bathrooms that *look* like they should also be in the wasteland. But I swear, everything is clean."

JJ went on to explain the bottom floor's layout, make a few excuses for her utter lack of progress on the house again and then showed Winnie to the bedroom.

"Is all this furniture yours? I thought it might be empty here." Winnie eyed the guest bedroom's yellow-painted iron-rod bed covered in a paisley bedspread.

JJ laughed a little at that.

"A few things are mine, but most of what you see came from Janice Wilkins," JJ answered. "Since she was downsizing and wanted to move quickly, she offered the furnishings and I agreed. It seemed like less hassle on my part at the time."

Price had fallen behind a little, but JJ could see him across the hall, peeking into the bonus room.

JJ's face flushed with heat.

"She even told me to keep a few things I didn't need," she said hurriedly. "Including a set of rusted dumbbells, a crib and a small collection of cow saltshakers."

Price had no doubt seen at least the first two of those items standing visible in the bonus room. The dumbbells were surprisingly compact. The crib was not.

Suddenly, JJ felt more self-conscious.

Thankfully, Price didn't hover.

He filled the doorframe and tapped his duffel bag.

"I'm curious about that saltshaker cow-thing, but first, let's get set up."

The next hour or so, Price did what Winnie had called a security reset. Security cameras and motion lights that he had brought were mounted outside in strategic places, new locks were installed on the front and back doors and sensors were placed along the seals of the windows on the first floor.

JJ was in awe of how thorough he was being. Though she wasn't sure it was necessary. Sheriff Weaver, Price and JJ had put their heads together for where they should lie low for a little while on the off chance that Lawson and his remaining men decided to strike again. His house was out of the question, the safe house the sheriff had used before had been taken off the market and JJ's house had also been put on the do-not-chance list. When the sheriff had realized that not even he knew where exactly JJ's work-in-progress home was, it convinced the three of them that Janice Wilkins's old home was the ticket.

"We don't know if Lawson, or whoever, even knows you were a part of what happened on the Becker Farm. But considering you went head-to-head with him at the convention center, I'm sure you're someone of interest to them," the sheriff had pointed out to her. "They may not make a move now that there's been a big fuss with two of their guys, but keeping the two people they'd probably use against Price *with* as far out of the way as we can is the best we can do."

Another one of those butterflies had fluttered its way around JJ's stomach at the mention of her being important to Price. She tried to remind herself that he was simply a good guy and proximity alone had gotten her the honor.

Still, she found herself fighting another wave of heat as he peeked his head around the kitchen door when he was finishing up and called her name.

"I could use your expertise real quick if you don't mind," he said. "Follow me outside."

JJ did. Each step after him she tried to remember what it felt like to wear the mask that had hidden her emotions as best she could.

That imaginary mask fell right back off when he took her by the shoulders and spun her back around to face the house. His hands were warm. She could feel them through the fabric of her shirt.

"Okay, Miss Sneak," he said. "Let's say you want to break into this bad boy. Show me all the ways you would so I can adjust my defenses if I need to."

JJ laughed.

"Wait? Is this what you think my expertise is? Sneaking?"

Price shrugged. He moved his hold from her shoulders to draping one arm around them, moving his body to her side. He was still facing the house.

"I'd actually say that your expertise is being surprising," he said. "Part of that charm just so happens to be getting into places with locked doors."

JJ was glad that his attention was elsewhere. There was no way her face wasn't the color of a stop sign.

"I think your expertise is making people with not-so-ordinary lives feel normal," she offered. "I once let it slip to my ex that I could theoretically hack into our university's website if I wanted, and it inspired a meltdown from him."

"Why?"

It was JJ's turn to shrug.

"I guess I ruined his image of me. Which is wild to me, considering the JJ Shaw he knew was a lot less reserved than the JJ Shaw in Seven Roads."

Price let out a sigh. It moved her body too.

"What can I say? Some people freak out a little when they realize they aren't the most interesting person in the room. That's why I always tell Winnie to never settle for someone who doesn't keep you guessing."

JJ already knew that Price was single. She had known

for a while, even before they had been thrown together. Yet her curiosity soared to the forefront and her question came out before she could think to censor it.

"Was her mom like that? Always keeping you guessing?"

Forget the stop-sign red. JJ felt like her face had gone directly into fire. She hadn't meant to overstep that far. She tried to backtrack in a flash.

"Sorry, that's too personal. I just haven't heard you or her or even Corrie talk about her, so I was just curious."

She glanced over to see the corner of Price's lips turn up.

"Don't apologize. I'd wonder too," he said. "As smart as Winnie's mom was, she was just as fun. Straight *A*s and straight chaos. She'd be the cool, calm, collected student at school and then would rope us into so many different kinds of shenanigans that not a day went by with her that I didn't feel like I was in some kind of sitcom." The smile didn't leave. It simply softened. "But then she got pregnant, and we had to really sit down and think about things. She's a good woman, but she never wanted to be a mom. That used to drive me up the wall, but now that I'm older and I've seen some things, I respect the resolve she had back then. She knew what she wanted, what she was capable of, and stuck to her guns. Then, on top of that, she gave me room to do the same. She never once pushed me to be a dad."

He patted himself on the chest in a teasing way, but JJ had a feeling he was being genuine.

"I chose that job myself. Pay's bad but I don't mind the work." His smile amped right back on up. "She still reaches out and emails with Winnie on occasion, but as far as interesting to me now, it's just not there. Not many people have had me on swivel either since we parted ways. Though I did date a lady who had a doll collection that took up *two* of her bedrooms a few years back. I bet she'd get a kick out of that cow shaker collection Ms. Wilkins left you."

Price laughed at his own comment. His arm was still around her. It was comfortable. *He* was comfortable.

And, apparently, to him JJ was interesting.

The thought warmed her.

It also saddened her.

She couldn't afford to be interesting anymore. Not until she could find her brother, stop Lawson and get herself into a position to keep the last of her family safe. No one could ever find out that Elle and Able Ortiz's children were alive.

Which was why JJ had decided long ago that she didn't have the luxury of a life for just her.

Interesting or not.

NIGHT FELL AND no one from the department or elsewhere made a peep. JJ and Winnie had put together an easy supper from what they had taken from their house and the three of them had enjoyed it while watching an HGTV show on Winnie's phone.

Price forgot for a bit that them being there wasn't exactly in their plans. It just felt nice and relaxing.

JJ fit in and that was nice.

It was also something that Winnie commented on after she had gotten ready for bed. Price sat on the ugly paisley duvet cover and watched as his daughter tried to find the right words.

"I know you told me that you aren't going to lie to me, but you aren't going to tell me the entire truth either. I just want to say, I hope whatever is going on with JJ that you help her fix it. I don't know what did it, but something about her is different. Like she isn't trying as hard anymore in general. And it's not like a bad thing. I actually like this version of her more." Winnie made a frustrated noise. "I guess what I'm trying to say is that I'd like to see more of this JJ, and I hope whatever had her so pinned up before gets straightened out. And that you're the one to help her do that."

Price's eyebrow rose sky-high at that.

"Me? Why me?"

At this, Winnie shrugged.

"Because you two are a good team."

It was a simple answer but one that sank heavy against Price. He told his daughter good-night and spent the next hour alone downstairs. It wasn't until he heard footfalls from the main bedroom that he decided that feeling needed some clarification.

He needed some clarification.

He took the stairs one at a time, but there was a new anxiousness in him. It was still there as he went past his daughter's closed door and still there when he lightly knocked on JJ's. Even after JJ opened the door and came into view, that feeling was still moving around there in his chest.

"We need to talk," he said.

There was no hope in the world for him, he'd realize later, after JJ nodded and then stepped aside.

"Come in."

Chapter Twenty

Price still had on his baseball shirt and jeans, but the look he was sporting now wasn't at all what JJ would describe as carefree. She stepped back another step after he closed the door behind him. He locked it too.

"What's wrong?" she asked, worried that she had somehow missed something and an attack was imminent.

Yet, the only target in his sights was her.

Price closed most of the distance between them in one clean stride. She noticed stubble along his jaw. She could smell some kind of spice from his skin. JJ had to tip her chin back a little just to look up into his eyes.

Why was he this close?

Did he think Winnie would overhear him and was trying for privacy?

She was at the other end of the hall with thick walls between her and them. Surely shutting the door had been enough.

Then again, maybe privacy wasn't at all on his mind.

When he spoke, his words were loud and clear.

"What about us?"

The volume and delivery might have been decisive, but JJ was as confused as ever.

"What about us?" she repeated.

Price gave one nod and brought his index finger to her shoulder. The small amount of pressure he placed there was brief but it sure did radiate after he pulled it back. He tapped himself next.

"You've got all of these plans on what to do to find your brother, what to do with Lawson and his group, and you even said you know what you want after it's all said and done, right?"

JJ nodded slowly.

"Yes. I don't want anyone to know my connection to him, to my parents."

"But you'll stay here? In Seven Roads, right?"

She nodded again.

"I don't think I could leave him after everything my parents went through."

"So, Seven Roads is settled then. You—this house?—is where you'll stay."

JJ was following the words, but she couldn't hang on to the feeling behind them. It felt...angry.

"That's the plan. Why? What's wrong?"

Price put his hands on his hips. It might have looked humorous had she understood what had inspired the now-obvious frustration.

"Winnie said something earlier and it got me thinking that...all these heavy things we've talked about, we never really hammered out the details of the *after*. I mean the brother thing, not wanting to reveal yourself, I get that. Though, to be honest, I was already trying to think of ways to persuade *you* to maybe rethink that too. But, that aside, I started thinking about all of these conversations with you. Then I started remembering your looks and then things that are *there* but not really there for you."

JJ knew her eyes had widened. He paused and searched

her face. Then he ran a hand down his own and dropped the other from his hip. She watched him turn around, take a few steps away, blow out a breath and come right back to the same spot so close to her.

"You smile, you say the words, but there's this—this space between them all," he continued. "You have convinced yourself that you *need* to keep up the life of the JJ Shaw who first came to Seven Roads to try and find her brother, but then I think you feel the *want* of actually living a life of this JJ Shaw. Of the woman who can hack into websites, fight close combat in elevators, make my kid laugh and fit right into my everyday life without so much as lifting a finger to try."

JJ didn't dare move.

Not even a blush stirred.

Price took another breath in but didn't walk away this time.

Instead, he shook his head.

"I realized just now that I think I know what you're going to do once we find your brother, and I'm hoping I'm wrong. So I'm asking again. What about us? What about me? What do you feel like you need to do if everything works out with Lawson and your brother? And, what about if it doesn't? Because, I'll be honest. I'm not like you, JJ. There's no space between I'm getting lost in. I know what I want, and I know what I need and it's one and the same."

His gaze dropped to her lips.

He watched her ask the only response she could manage in the moment.

"And what's that?"

He put his hand against her cheek. His eyes didn't leave her lips.

"You."

They hadn't talked about their first kiss even once after it happened in the department bathroom. A part of JJ had wanted to. A part hadn't. It had been an intense day and emotions were running high and he had comforted her. That was it, right?

She had needed that answer.

She hadn't wanted it.

Price was right. There was that space in between the two lives she had been living.

Price was also warm.

His lips connected for another kiss. There was no denying this time everything was different.

Price pressed his body flush against hers. He tilted her head back slightly and paused. JJ realized he was waiting for her to accept him or reject him.

There was no getting lost in between for her anymore.

JJ applied her own pressure against his lips, against his body. That was all the man needed. His tongue parted her lips, and their kiss went from a solitary instance to an all-consuming constant. JJ's hands wound their way up his neck and tangled in his hair. Price's hands cradled and roamed until they were no longer standing.

The bed in the main room was firm. It didn't give as Price laid her down its middle, it didn't cave as he started to take off their clothes and it didn't buckle as she arched against his fingers sliding between her underwear and skin. He maneuvered inside of her with one hand and adjusted her against him with the other.

JJ moved against his mouth.

He held her close, working until she couldn't take it anymore.

Then he adjusted again.

This time JJ helped.

She returned in kind and stripped him until there was nothing between their bodies but heat and sweat.

Price had already made it clear that he was a fan but feeling him against her was an experience that excited her to no end. When they were done with the appetizers, he devoured the main course. She used the last of her willpower to not call out as he pushed deep inside of her.

There was no space between them at all after that.

PRICE WOKE UP feeling good.

Well, not all good. He was sore in spots from his fight the day before and from the party, but who cared about some bruises and pulled muscles? He felt good on good, and he knew exactly why.

He rolled over, ready to cuddle up to a Miss JJ Shaw. Instead, he grabbed at a whole bunch of empty space.

Price popped up like a daisy in spring.

He palmed his phone on the nightstand, hoping there were no security alerts that he had somehow slept through, but heard an explanation for the lack of JJ.

He heard water sloshing from the bedroom's attached bathroom and let out a breath of relief.

Then he got to smiling again.

Price rolled out of bed and went to knock on the bathroom door.

"Yeah?" JJ called.

"Can I come in?" he asked, hand already on the doorknob. He waited though as she took a beat to respond.

"Um, sure."

The bathroom was full of steam. The bathtub was full of JJ and bubbles.

Price eyed both with a grin.

JJ's face was already flushed from the heat, but he

thought he might have seen it turn a deeper shade of red. She collected an island of bubbles and pulled them closer to her chest.

"I know we showered last night but, well, I felt like I needed this too."

Price laughed and put his hands up in defense.

"Hey, I'm not judging your need to soak. In fact, the idea doesn't sound half bad…"

He nodded to the spot opposite her.

She shook her head but laughed.

"I don't think so, sir. You're just going to have to wait your turn. I'm a one-person bath kind of woman. Especially when this woman is in desperate need of Icy Hot on several places." That blush seemed to flare to life again. She lowered her voice a little. "Plus, I'm not pushing my luck with Winnie being around. I don't know about you, but I'm not that eager to scar a teenager like that."

Price laughed.

"I guess you're not wrong there," he said. "Can I at least chat with you while you soak?"

JJ looked surprised.

"Chat with me?"

"Yeah. Like you said, I like talking. I especially like talking to you. Can I sit?"

That surprise was still there but she nodded.

"Just don't try any funny business. This is a casual, platonic soak."

Price pulled his towel off of the rack and folded it into a seat next to her on the tile. It made him a good height to lean his elbow on the lip of the tub. He put his head on his hand and stared across the water at said casual, platonic soaker.

JJ rolled her eyes.

"Maybe saying yes was a bad idea," she commented.

Price shrugged.

"I'm just admiring the view, is all. Can't blame a guy for that."

Where he thought she might complain once more, JJ simply rolled her eyes again. A small smile played at her lips though.

It was nice to see her like this.

Not the naked part, not the vulnerable part.

It was the trusting that had him feeling all types of ways.

JJ Shaw had opened up to him about her past, she had let him into her bed, but neither was a promise to let anything else happen past that. He'd asked her about them, about her future plans, but he hadn't gotten an answer. Not a verbal one at least.

Her letting him sit there now meant more to him than she knew.

Because the choices she was making now had nothing to do with Lawson Cole, the search for her brother or keeping her secret identity safe.

It was just a woman soaking in a bubble bath, talking to a man who had fallen for her all while sitting on damp tile in his boxers.

Because, while he hadn't spelled it out to a tee, Price had also realized that he had fallen for JJ Shaw.

Straight to the bottom of the bottom.

Did JJ return his feelings?

He wasn't sure how much.

He also decided not to push her right now to ask.

Especially after catching sight of something he'd already seen in bed the night before.

It was the same scar he had seen before they had left for the party. Angry, shining, and most likely undeniably painful when it had first happened.

A scar from the accident.

It sobered Price a bit, though he made sure to keep a small smile on.

Maybe it wasn't enough.

JJ went from bantering and dove right into the complicated world outside of the bathroom walls around them.

"You never asked who my source was," she said. "I feel wrong somehow not telling you, now with everything we've been through."

"You don't have to," he pointed out.

She didn't hesitate.

"It's Riker. My godfather. I can't remember if I told you or not, but when I went off to college, he married a really nice woman who ended up needing to take care of her parents. So they moved out of state and they're still out there being all cute and happy." She sighed. It moved some of the bubbles nearest her mouth. "It's why I never told Riker about Mr. Cole coming to see me. Why I never told him about Mom surviving and having my brother. Why I never told him the real reason I left the city for a small town I'd only visited once or twice. He just—he just has a lot of guilt for what happened, a lot of regrets. I know, because we both tried to work on our feelings about everything through the years. He eventually said he found peace, but I know it eats him up that we never got the justice my parents deserved."

She started to swirl some of the bubbles around. Her eyes stayed on them as she continued.

"I didn't want to tell him what I'd been up to until I had it all sorted. I wanted to keep him in his peace as much as possible. But, if anyone could identify someone from the group, or know a different source that could, it's him. And since they might try and use Winnie against you, I didn't want to just wait and hope. So, yesterday I sent him pictures and described the men. Said they were working for Lawson Cole and asked if he could help."

"What did he say?"

She kept swirling.

"He had a lot of questions, but I told him I didn't have the time. That I was okay, and I'd explain everything once he got back to me. I told him I needed it fast. Then he said fine, he loved me and to stay safe." She sighed again. "A part of me wanted to keep him out of this forever because I know once he finds out about Mom still being alive…he's going to run himself into the ground with guilt, even though I don't think anyone would blame him for what happened."

"Just remind him that he saved a hurt, terrified kid and bluffed a powerful man into giving that girl a safe life to live. He did good."

JJ nodded.

"He did. But the second he finds out about my brother, he won't just keep living the life he has now. He'll rush back here and join the fight. He'll leave his happy, safe life and, well, that hurts my heart if I'm being honest."

Price reached his hand out and took JJ's in his. He let it sink a little in the warm water. Her dark eyes found his and sunk there too.

"You don't need to worry about everything and everyone all at once," he said. "You also can't control or predict how people will feel. Let's work with what we have, let's deal with the now, and I promise you what comes next, I'll help you with. Okay?"

With his other hand, he tapped the bottom of her chin and smiled.

"Soak in the tub, not in what-ifs."

It took a few moments, but JJ cracked a smile.

"That was incredibly cheesy, Deputy Collins."

He shrugged.

"Doesn't mean it wasn't true."

She admitted he was right, and their conversation went to the bathroom around them, then the house renovations as a whole. It was normal and comfortable. JJ also held his hand the entire time.

It wasn't until she was finished, dried and dressed that Price made his way down to the kitchen to start breakfast. Winnie was just waking up and JJ stopped in her room to chat. He smiled as he descended the stairs to the sound of them talking in the background.

That smile was still playing at his lips when an alert on his phone and a text came in at the same time.

It was the sheriff. He was outside and wanted to talk.

Price didn't waste time. He threw on his boots and was at the sheriff's truck in a flash.

Liam looked like he hadn't slept much. He had a sandwich bag in his hand and threw it to Price when he was close enough.

"I went to Josiah's to have another look around to see if there was anything we might have missed. I found that in his room. I saw its partner yesterday or else I wouldn't have thought anything about it."

Price knew instantly what the small item inside the bag was.

An earring.

A blue one. Identical to the one JJ had on the day before. Price had meant to ask her where the missing one had gone but so much had already been happening.

Including Price's decision to keep JJ's search through Josiah Teller's house a secret.

He opened his mouth now to say *something*, but the sheriff cut him off.

"I'm not here to talk about that. I'm here to talk about the man who JJ fought in the woods." He let out a long, dragging breath. That tired came out strong with it. "He succumbed to his injuries late last night."

Price felt cold.

"He died," he said bluntly.

The sheriff nodded.

"That in itself would be a lot, especially for JJ, even though it was self-defense, but something else happened."

Price's already-bad feeling only deepened.

Hearing the words only added anger into it.

"Your neighbors called in about half an hour ago. Someone tore up your house, Price. And they left a message behind."

Price was seeing red, but he managed to read the note from the picture Liam held up for him.

He read it aloud, fire and ice in his veins.

"'A life for a life. Your daughter's next.'"

Chapter Twenty-One

Life got fast. Real fast.

Deputy Little and Deputy Gavin came out to the house and then the former Sheriff Trouble, Liam's wife, came too. It was one thing to bluff about having Winnie Collins. It was another to threaten her.

Price was at the helm of their meetings that took place in the dining room. JJ took part at first, but she had found herself in the bonus room, idly staring. It was only when Winnie came in after a while that JJ realized she had made a decision.

It wasn't a want.

It wasn't a need.

It was a *must*.

Still, JJ's feet were slow about it.

Maybe it was that space in between again that Price had talked about. She was getting lost in it.

She couldn't keep that going for too long though.

Seeing Winnie pretend to not be scared was a good reminder of that.

"Did you get kicked out too?" The teenager pointed down at the floor. The kitchen wasn't far off from their spot above. "I tried to join, and Dad used his cop voice on me. I appreciate that he never lies to me, but it still feels like I'm missing out on some things I might need to know."

Winnie came to a stop next to JJ. She was standing next to the crib of all things. Winnie peered over the edge and at the cow saltshaker collection that was resting inside. She didn't seem to need JJ to respond. She went on, just like her father did.

"This isn't the first time that he's been nervous, but I think that's when Dad really shines. I know he can be lame and goofy and sometimes just won't leave you alone, but he's also really good at his job. He's really good at keeping people safe. So, I wouldn't worry too much. He'll figure it all out."

JJ's heart tore.

She looked over at the girl, who was light-years ahead of her age.

There she was, trying to comfort JJ when it was JJ's fault she was the one being threatened.

A life for a life.

JJ had no doubt that it had been Lawson behind that message, using his father's old adage and twisting it for revenge.

Because the man *she* had fought in the woods had died.

No matter which way JJ looked at the situation, she was the cause of the trouble now in Seven Roads.

She was the reason Price's daughter—the person he loved most in the world—had gotten a death threat by the same people who had killed her father. Who had tried to kill her. Who now wanted to kill her brother.

JJ didn't ball her hand into a fist because she didn't want to damage what was resting on her palm. Instead, she looked at it for what felt like the hundredth time since Price had slyly given it to her without a second thought.

Winnie inclined her head to look.

"Oh, that's pretty," she said.

JJ smiled. It was one of the few she truly felt.

"Isn't it? My mom actually made it for me all by herself." She laughed. "This was actually the third attempt. My mom was really, really not a crafty person. It was a rule in my house that me and Dad wrapped all the presents and made the birthday banners and did anything that included tape, glue or having to deal with a billion little pieces."

JJ moved the earring closer so Winnie could see it better.

"So when she gave these to me for my tenth birthday, I really understood how special they were," she continued. "Then, when my dad let me know that she had been trying to make the perfect pair for weeks, I decided right then and there that *these* were my favorite pair of earrings that I'd ever own."

She ran a finger over the scratch mark that split the worn flower painted on the side.

"You see this scratch?" she asked. "Dad told me that she almost threw the whole thing away because she thought it ruined it. But Dad, knowing just how to make my mom feel better about anything, convinced her that *this* scratch is what makes these earrings so valuable. 'It's an Elle exclusive. The rarest of rare. No one else in the entire world will ever have this.'"

That smile started to slip away.

Winnie didn't notice.

Instead, she was impressed.

"I can't believe you still have them after all these years. Dad got me a pearl bracelet last Christmas and I still haven't been able to find where I lost it in my room."

JJ stopped rubbing the side of the earring.

Despite herself, despite her resolve, JJ told Winnie Collins something that no one else in the entire world knew. Not even her father.

"I actually did lose this," she said. "I was wearing them

when I was in a car accident when I was ten. The other one, I still wear when I'm missing my mom. It wasn't until today that I got this one back."

Winnie's eyebrow rose.

"How?"

JJ's smile was gone.

"My best guess is that Mom wanted it to find me again."

JJ had been looking for a sign, for a lead, for anything that would lead her to the truth. To her family.

She thought it only fitting that, in the end, it was her mom who would lead her to her brother.

JJ took the other earring out of her ear. She pulled on one last smile and turned to Winnie.

"I'm really awful at keeping track of things. Do you think you could hold on to these for me until your dad has everything taken care of? It would help me feel less nervous knowing they're somewhere safe."

Thankfully, Winnie didn't know the full extent of what was going on. She didn't question the request. Instead, she looked suddenly determined.

"Don't worry. I won't lose them like the pearls. You can count on me."

JJ ran her finger over the scratch one last time before handing both earrings over.

"I'm actually going to go lie down for a little bit," JJ said once they were in Winnie's hand. "I didn't get much sleep last night. Do you think if your dad comes up here, you could tell him I'm sorry?"

Winnie snorted, eyes on the earrings.

"Sorry for what? Napping? Don't worry. Dad has definitely taken his fair share of naps. Plus, if he's not going to let us in on the talks downstairs, what else can we do?" She waved the concern off. "Go nap. I got you."

JJ wavered right then and there.

She wanted to say more, but knew too much might make the girl suspicious.

So, JJ went to her bedroom and shut the door behind her.

A MANHUNT TURNED Seven Roads upside down. Still, as it became afternoon, no one could find Lawson Cole. It was frustrating. It was enraging.

It finally made Price feel like he had done enough for the moment to deserve a break to check on JJ. Since giving her the news that the man she had fought had died, he'd seen a change in her so drastic that he had done the only thing he could in a time like that.

He had given her space.

Now he wanted that space to disappear. He wanted to check on her, he wanted to be near her. He wanted to sit next to her, hold her hand and talk out the situation. Then he wanted to make her and Winnie something good to eat. After that? They could figure out their next steps.

He told his friends downstairs that he would be right back and went to Winnie's room first. She had her door open and was sprawled out on her bed, reading a book. Price paused to take in the sight. He remembered when she was half that size, begging him to read her favorite kids' book about learning numbers by counting sheep.

Price was about to say just that when he noticed something lying next to the book.

"Are those JJ's earrings?" he asked instead.

Winnie jumped in surprise but recovered with a scowl on her face. She scooped the earrings up and dramatically placed them against her chest.

"They are and, before you say anything, I already promised to keep them safe. And that this isn't the same as the pearl situation so before you say anything—"

"Keep them safe?" he interrupted. "She asked you to keep them safe?"

Winnie nodded.

"Her mom made them for her and, well, she didn't say it, but I think her mom is gone so they mean a lot." She held one out to him and pointed to something across its surface. "She said her mom handmade them for her, but she lost one in an accident. *Then* she found this one today. Now she's worried in all of this going on that she might lose them again."

Price had been about to take the one held out to him.

He paused the move midair.

"What?" was all he could manage.

Winnie saw the change in him. Her answer was slower but still she didn't understand.

"I think she gave them to me because she's trying to keep me distracted," she admitted. "She didn't really seem that stressed when we talked earlier. Maybe she thought I was."

Price started to backtrack through the door. He stared down the hall.

JJ's bedroom door was closed.

Adrenaline poured through him as he took each step closer to it.

He heard Winnie follow him. She whisper-yelled out.

"Don't wake her up! She said she was going to nap."

Price shook his head.

He already knew what he would find once he opened the door.

Or, rather, who he wouldn't.

Still, he held out some hope.

That hope didn't last.

Once the door was open, it was easy to see the room was empty.

Winnie bumped into him.

"What else did she say?" he asked, striding across the room to the bathroom, just in case.

It was also empty.

Winnie looked confused.

"Nothing. She said she was going to take a nap and that she was sorry."

Price turned at that.

"She was sorry?"

Winnie nodded.

"She told me to tell you she was sorry…" Winnie's confusion started to turn to realization that she had missed something important. "I—I thought she meant she was sorry that she was going to take a nap."

Price cussed low and checked the room for anything that might tell him that he was wrong. When he couldn't find anything, he pulled out his phone and started to call JJ.

"Dad!"

Price hurried to the bathroom. Winnie pointed into the trash can as the call went to voicemail immediately.

He didn't have to wonder why.

In the trash can was JJ's phone.

Smashed to pieces.

That was the last nail in the coffin.

Price didn't stay still after that.

He ran down the stairs, Winnie right behind him.

Once he got everyone's attention in the dining room, he whirled around and looked his daughter right in the eye.

"I love you, but I have to go and help JJ right now," he told her.

Fear etched itself into Winnie's expression. Price hated it. He knocked her forehead twice with a gentle rap.

"I wouldn't leave you if I thought you were in danger. But, JJ is. And, like you said, she and I are a really good team. When I'm in trouble, she saves me. When she's in trouble, I save her. Those are the rules. Okay?"

Before she could say anything, he turned to Liam's wife, Blake. She stood between Deputy Gavin and Rose.

"I don't think Lawson will come after us anymore, but just in case, can you please keep my daughter safe?"

Blake, mother to three and fierce protector to any and all of those in need, nodded on reflex.

"Update Liam in the car," she ordered instead of questioning him. "We're good here."

He nodded, grateful.

He turned back to Winnie.

Price would never forget the first time he ever saw his daughter. She was impossibly small, and he was incredibly afraid. Now, she was almost an adult. Still, that fear always stayed.

In that moment, though, his daughter gave him something else. Something that he realized he needed from her before he could go.

She gave him permission to leave her.

"Go save the day, Dad."

He didn't need anything more. Price was in his truck and flying down the road in what felt like one fluid movement. He put the sheriff on speaker just as he was tearing out of the neighborhood.

"Lawson Cole doesn't need to use Winnie anymore."

The sheriff didn't make him repeat it.

"Why?" he asked instead. "What happened?"

Price thought of the earrings. The blue one with a scratch.

He thought of her telling Winnie she was sorry to him.

He slammed his hands on the steering wheel as he answered.

"Because JJ is making a mighty move and turning herself in to him."

The sheriff was all alarm. It had nothing on the storm of emotions raging within Price.

"Why would she do that?" Liam asked.

Price cussed low.

"Because she finally found her brother," he said. "It's Josiah Teller."

He had no doubt that now JJ knew, she was going to sacrifice herself to keep Josiah safe.

And Price couldn't—wouldn't—let that happen.

Chapter Twenty-Two

JJ had exactly two cards left to play.

The first was the obvious one. The card she knew she would most likely play in the end.

Josiah Teller was her brother. She had found him all thanks to the earring her mother must have left with him before she passed. JJ didn't need any more proof. She didn't need to see him again, to talk to him. She had been lucky enough to already share a few conversations with him during the week he had been in the hospital.

She also took to heart the fact that without meaning to, she had already saved her brother when she had found him in the field. Everything after had been bonus.

It also made her heart soften a little more to realize that the man seemed to have had a happy life before trouble had found him. She had been through his house—though maybe not as thoroughly as she would have liked—and seen a life well-lived through the years.

Pictures of people smiling, hugging and celebrating. He had hobbies. Art supplies had filled his guest bedroom, something that now made JJ smile. It would have tickled their mother to know that despite her lack of patience with arts and crafts, her son seemed to thrive at it. He also seemed to be a fan of reading, something their father had been avid at. She hadn't been able to search all the books, but it looked like he tended to gravitate toward science fiction. Something that JJ actually loved herself.

It was a small thing, but it felt like a lot at the same time.

Josiah was a little bit of all of them, even if he didn't know.

JJ took that solace with her to play that first card.

Like Riker before her, she would try to make a deal with a Cole to keep the people she loved out of harm's way. Winnie, to be exact. Price by extension.

No one would ever need to know that Elle and Able Ortiz had had two children. Once JJ gave herself up, that was it.

Price wouldn't be happy but she was confident that, no matter what, he would keep Josiah a secret too. He would look out for him as well. Maybe that was why JJ had told Winnie the story of the earrings. She wanted to leave a breadcrumb or two so Price would find his way to her brother.

He's going to be so mad at you, JJ thought.

But JJ had already decided to play the second card, and once she did, there was no turning back.

JJ walked up to the Colt Bar and Grill's front door. They weren't open yet but the sign on the door said they would be in two months. There was a grand opening party being planned too.

JJ took a quick look around the building and parking lot. It wasn't remote but the establishments closest to them was a gas station and a Subway that faced the opposite direction. Two cars were in the lot. She had snuck out of her house with a bike she'd kept in the back. That bike she looked at once more before she knocked on the tinted door.

It wasn't long before that door opened.

A man she had never seen before gruffly told her that they were closed.

She sighed.

"I need to talk to Lawson Cole," she said. "If he's here, let him know that JJ Shaw has some information."

The burly man wasn't a talker. He also didn't need her to keep prying. He disappeared behind the door for a minute or two before opening back up. This time, he stepped aside to let her in.

The building was surprisingly open for what it was. JJ wasn't a pro at renovations, but she had to believe no progress had been made to the structure in years. The bones of a restaurant were there but everything was worn, covered in dust and in obvious disuse. She was surprised this was where Lawson was holed up. Though, when the burly man took her down a hallway and into a room at the back, she admitted to herself that this fit him in a way.

Potential on the outside but rotted on the inside.

At least the storage room seemed to have been dusted. It was also set up to look more like a lounge. There were still shelving with boxes and plastic tubs close to the back wall, but the rest of the space had tables and chairs, two couches, and an area that looked like it had been used to make simple meals. There were two other doors at the end of the room, but both were closed. JJ didn't have the time or the mental bandwidth to wonder about what was behind them. Her attention went right to the man sitting at the table in the center of everything.

Lawson Cole had his head tilted a little in smug curiosity. Like the cat had been delivered his mouse. It was only icing on the cake that the mouse had delivered itself. He leaned forward. He was wearing a suit.

She wasn't a fan.

"JJ Shaw, I almost didn't recognize you without you bouncing around an elevator." He looked to the burly guy behind her but addressed her still. "Should I be expecting our Deputy Collins and the sheriff department soon, or are they already lurking around outside?"

Based on the lack of fear in him, JJ assumed he had an exit strategy just in case. Or maybe he had more people hidden in the building, waiting for his word. Either way, he was too calm for her liking.

Though, maybe that was his ego.

If someone thought they were untouchable long enough, they probably couldn't help but believe they were.

"It's just me," JJ assured him. "No one even knows I'm here, especially not Deputy Collins."

The burly man must have shown that she was, it appeared, alone.

Lawson smiled. It was all snake.

"Then, I have to ask a few questions, first—"

JJ raised her hands and turned around to face the burly man.

"Check me," she ordered. "No weapons, no phone, no wire. No anything."

The man really was a simple guy. He did as she said without comment. Lawson had stopped though. His eyebrow was high. JJ's patience was low. When his lackey was done and gave the thumbs-up, JJ walked over and took the seat opposite Lawson at the table. It put them only a few feet apart.

The closer proximity made her feel sick with disgust.

She cut to the chase.

"You're going to ask how I found you next and then why I'm here, I'm sure," she started. "So let me answer." JJ held up her index finger. "The man who attacked me in the woods wasn't identified but I figured someone from your group had to have confirmed his death to give you the whole *life for a life* excuse and escalation for Deputy Collins and his daughter. So I hacked into the hospital's security system and, in what I can only say is a disappointing lack of self-awareness on his part, found a man sneaking into the morgue in the basement. I took a leap of faith and tracked him to the parking lot where I was able to find out that he had taken a cab, of all things, here. I'm not sure what you're paying these guys, but may I suggest in the future going the extra mile for a vehicle that isn't as easy to track."

She held up a second finger and continued to back talk the man as much as she could.

"Which brings me to say I want to make a deal and I want to make it fast before someone else figures out you're here."

Lawson's smile had dropped a little. He was irritated.

"A deal?" he asked. "Let me guess. You want me to back off your dear deputy and his daughter? What could you even offer me to make that remotely enticing?"

There was no reason to beat around the bush.

JJ dove right in.

"I'm offering you me." She held up her hand to stop his, no doubt, snarky remark. "And before you turn that down, I should let you know that I know you're looking for Able Ortiz's son."

It was a complete and utter change.

Lawson really had had no clue that JJ was involved.

No more snake smile.

"But, I have to say, you got one thing wrong about this entire thing," she added before he could cut in. JJ touched her chest. "Your father not only kept it a secret, he kept *me* a secret. I'm the daughter you're looking for. Able and Elle Ortiz never produced a son."

His eyes widened.

"Their daughter died in the car accident," he said. "The mother survived with an unborn child."

"That's what you've *heard*, but have you ever seen proof? Or do you think it was something your father said to try and cover for me one last time before he died?"

That's when JJ finally knew what she suspected all this time to be true.

Lawson Cole truly had no proof that her mother had survived and had a child. It had been a rumor, a rumor that had been the truth, but nothing he could have verified.

So JJ's plan was going to work.

She could cover up the existence of Josiah once and for all right here. She leaned into it to make sure the job was done well.

"I came back here to live a nice life in a place my mother used to love and then, one day, I see you bouncing around here and suddenly men who would have been the same age as that unborn child—with adoption stories to boot—start getting into trouble." She shook her head. "I guess I'm like my dad. I couldn't just let that sit. I thought I could finish what he started."

She sighed. It wasn't an act.

"But then you put me in a tough spot and went for an innocent girl. I realized that I wasn't willing to bet her life on the fact that I could win against you. If only for the logistics."

Lawson's voice was tight.

"Logistics?" he repeated.

JJ nodded.

"You have more people than me. Plain and simple. So,

I'm here to take the loss instead of dragging anyone else through this mess. So, let's end this now."

To his credit, Lawson seemed to be taking the news in stride.

He recovered faster than she thought he would.

"If all of this is true, what kind of deal are you offering? Your life for the deputy's daughter's?"

This was the part that would lead to her end.

If there was more time, if she had been more sure of his numbers and what information he did and didn't have, JJ might not have given in as easily.

But she believed she had finally hit a dead end she couldn't come back from.

JJ thought about her mother, all alone before she died. She thought about her father, dedicating his entire life to helping others. She thought about Riker, giving up his everything to keep her safe and loved and happy. She thought of Josiah, happy that their family would live on no matter what happened to her. She thought of Winnie, holding her mother's earrings.

She thought of Price, holding her hand in the middle of bubbles.

JJ smiled.

Lawson leaned in just a little more. He was all ears.

Which was good. She needed him to really believe her. So she told her last lies, her last truths and the last deal she would ever make.

"I am the evidence against your group. I am the only one in existence that knows enough about you to destroy you. So, once you deal with me, there's no reason for you to ever come back here again. There's no reason for you to hurt or harass anyone else here, because all it will end up doing is putting a brand-new target on your back. And, if you really want to be the new boss calling all the shots, getting all that new attention would only make your cousin seem all the stronger. Dealing with me? That will cement your spot against him. And isn't that what you really want?"

That was it.

JJ closed her mouth.

The deed was done.

And, by the look on Lawson's face, he had already made his decision well before he said it out loud.

"I guess it's only fair to accept," he said. "A life for a life, after all."

Chapter Twenty-Three

Lawson might have accepted the deal but that didn't mean he was ready to button it up and call it a day. He turned his head and shouted toward one of the closed doors with notable glee.

"Boys? Why don't you come out so we can all chat." Lawson turned back to her, his eyebrow raised again. "Wait. I do have a question you didn't answer in that way-too-wordy speech you just gave."

He pointed at his face and made a disgusting pout to seem cute.

"How exactly did you know about me when you saw me at the party? I'm fairly certain your father's intel didn't include me yet. Like you, my father also kept me hidden until I was older."

JJ knew it wasn't the time or place, but what else did she have to lose?

She smirked and was about to tell him another secret she had guarded well through the years.

But, behind him, the world shifted.

The door he had called out to opened.

However, the boys he had been calling weren't the ones who appeared.

JJ tried her very best to keep her face the exact same it had been before she recognized the two men. She might not have kept talking had she not realized that the burly man, who she believed to have been behind her, had been gone for a bit.

So, to stall, she continued.

"When I was sixteen, I found your father and then tracked him to a funeral he was attending for someone in your group. I stayed on the outskirts, trying to figure out how many of you there were and realized we were sorely outmatched. Then I saw you, standing at his side in a suit even then."

JJ felt the old anger from the past flare anew.

"After that, I made sure every plan I made included ways to destroy you too. But I was told to take a breath by a god-father who wanted a much better life for me."

That anger washed away. JJ felt a different kind of warmth in its place. One born from patience, love and understanding.

"Honestly, I guess he's the reason you and I are both here right now," JJ added. She turned to one of the men behind Lawson. He was the older of the two, weathered but not worn.

"Does a life for a life apply here?" she asked him.

Riker smiled.

"That's definitely something we should talk about."

All hell broke loose within the next minute.

The burly man came back and stayed as simple as before. He ran right at the first person he could, just as Lawson reminded them that he did indeed have *some* skill. He threw himself backward and started fighting Riker, a blessing in itself since the fight would have already been over had Riker had a good shot.

JJ couldn't track that line of the fight too long. Her attention diverted to her immediate problem. The burly man was back and unavoidable. She braced herself for an impact that would at the very least break some bones.

It never came.

The man was stopped in his tracks by a hit that was so loud it seemed to vibrate through the space around them.

And Price kept going.

Hits were doled out in an impressive flurry against the bigger man, making Price look like a man possessed. They targeted his chest, side, and finished with a one-two wallop against the man's head. JJ could only watch in awe as Mr. Burly went from as formidable as a wall to as placid as a doormat.

JJ watched as Price's bloodied knuckles brushed against the man's collar while checking to see if he was faking it or really unconscious.

The man was liquid.

He was out.

Price's gaze swiveled to hers in the next instant but there wasn't time to say a thing.

Lawson had gotten out of Riker's reach, and it was clear he had a new target in mind.

JJ went from bracing against a potential attack from the burly man to barely being able to lift her forearms up against the new frightening attacker.

Unlike the man before, Lawson was going to make it to her.

JJ saw his fist incoming and knew there was enough torque behind it to do an unsettling amount of damage. He was already upon her as she gritted her teeth.

But so was Price.

Large, quick hands wrapped around her biceps and pulled her backwards just as Lawson's hit landed against her forearm. Pain lit across her, but she knew the quick movement back had saved her from absorbing the entire force. JJ, never a woman to let go of control, melted into Price's plan with absolutely no fight.

She let herself be slung back even further while Price replaced her position between him and Lawson with nothing but righteous anger. JJ stumbled several steps away from the new match up.

There she watched the man she had fallen in love with deliver a bone-crunching punch to the man she had spent years hating. Lawson let out a scream that gurgled as blood gushed from his nose.

That's when she saw the gun in his other hand.

This is what JJ would think back on later as the downfall of Lawson Cole. A perfect example of his unchecked ego.

Riker hadn't been able to take his gun away.

She definitely hadn't had the chance either.

So, why hadn't he used it against her when the opening had been there? Why, instead, had he come at her with his fists?

Was it out of anger?

Did he want to feel her hurt personally?

Or had he simply forgotten in the rush of the fighting that he had had a trump card that would have ended her?

JJ would never know and, in the moment she clocked the gun, she wouldn't have the time to wonder.

Instead, only fear had taken over.

Not for her, but for Price standing between them.

JJ wanted to yell, to do something to stop the quick aiming of Lawson's gun, but there was no time.

Thankfully, Riker had been forgotten.

And he was right on time.

Instead of using his gun to end the man who had given them such grief, JJ's godfather used his weapon as a bat.

He swung the handgun down with the strength of a man who had been waiting over a decade to get justice.

There was nothing any of them could do but watch it happen.

And watch JJ did.

Lawson Cole crumpled to the ground, blood across his face from Price, and a hit from Riker that might have killed him.

His suit, always immaculate, was stained red.

JJ found her footing again, easier this time. Her forearms hurt and the burly man near her wasn't moving at all. Riker was heaving in breaths, his eyebrow busted and part of his shirt torn.

Price's knuckles were busted and bloodied, but he used one of those hands to give her a thumbs up with a surprisingly cheeky smile. Amongst the chaos and adrenaline-filled people still standing, he delivered a one-liner that pulled a genuine laugh from her.

"I don't think I ever told you, but I'm also actually really good at fighting."

Chapter Twenty-Four

Four months later and Price was still mad.

"I already said I was sorry. *And* that I won't ever do it again."

JJ was sitting shotgun in his parked truck, wearing a dress with daisies on it and a look of reproach that matched the expression of the girl sitting behind her.

"Yeah, Dad. She's already apologized a ton," Winnie added. "Also, you have to remember she only sacrificed herself because she wanted to make super sure that you and me were safe. And her brother. Her *only family left after her tragedy.*"

Winnie was overly dramatic with the last part, but his girlfriend in the passenger's seat really ate it up.

She gave him the big doe eyes and nodded.

"Next time I feel outnumbered by an anonymous criminal organization trying to find and destroy everyone I love, I won't sacrifice myself," she said. "At least, not without checking with you first. Okay?"

Price narrowed his eyes but couldn't deny that he liked hearing JJ put him and Winnie on the list of people she loved.

He also couldn't fully blame her for what she had done, especially since they realized their situation had been a lot more dire than originally believed.

Lawson Cole's nameless organization hadn't just been one branch on a small tree. His ego had been somewhat warranted. Aside from the men Price had fought alongside Riker, there had been more lying in wait. It wasn't until Lawson himself started turning on his group that everyone realized just how outnumbered they had been.

Still, that didn't mean Price would ever fully be okay with JJ going off into danger alone.

Though, to be fair, she hadn't so much as left his side or Winnie's for more than a few hours since then. They had gone from partners to a unit of three.

Well, three plus the occasional fourth.

"Alright, alright, I guess as long as you check with me, I'll try not to bring it up every time we come here," Price said now, motioning to the house past his windshield.

"That would be nice, considering we come here every Sunday for dinner," Winnie said.

Price let out a long sigh.

"If you two keep ganging up on me, I'm going to have to rethink our futures. Specifically, this whole *combining households* thing. You two against me *and* a house renovation? I don't think I can take it."

Winnie rolled her eyes and opened the truck door. She patted him on the shoulder before jumping out.

"Don't act like you don't love it, Dad."

She was off in a flash, running up Josiah's driveway with a laugh.

JJ stayed in her seat. Price did too. He could tell she was nervous about the day they had ahead of them. He simply waited for her to say so. She did after a moment.

"I guess it doesn't feel real sometimes. Being here, being able to do this with them."

Price knew what she meant. Being at Josiah's was nothing new, at least not in the last four months. Ever since Price and Riker had convinced her to talk to Josiah. To tell him about his biological family.

She had asked for Price to be with her when she sat Josiah down, and that was how he became the second person to realize that Lawson Cole had been right. The key to finding Able Ortiz's evidence against his group had been his son all along.

But, it had been Elle Ortiz who had been the one to lead them to it.

Josiah's adoptive parents hadn't simply been strangers that had wound up with him. Instead, his adoptive mother had been a nurse at a scared Elle Ortiz's hospital bedside as her health declined. In the little time she had left, she had convinced the young couple to not only adopt her son, but to keep his origins a secret. Then, with the money given to her in guilt by Lawson Cole's father, she had orchestrated an airtight paper trail that would purposely throw off anyone who might come looking.

But, her last and most heartfelt request had been kept in a small wooden box with a few keepsakes she was promised would stay with her son.

The first had been Able Ortiz's wedding band.

The second had been Elle Ortiz's engagement ring.

The third had been Lydia Ortiz's earring.

The fourth had been a key. She hadn't known what it belonged to but had believed it was important.

And it had been, but only one person had been able to figure out where it led.

Riker Shaw hadn't been able to save his best friend or his wife, but he had been the one to figure out Able Ortiz's makeshift hiding place for all the evidence against the Coles' organization. It had taken a month to track down, but he had done it. Not only was the group being dismantled, the growth that had happened after Able's passing had been halted by the fact that Lawson was giving everyone's secrets away for his attempt at a lighter sentence.

JJ had mused one night that, in the end, he had become the most destructive evidence against himself.

She wasn't wrong.

The investigation was still ongoing but the fear that they would become targets had gone. That was largely thanks to a deal struck to keep the Ortiz family's and Riker's names out of everything attached to it. The last deal that Riker Shaw made for his best friend's family.

JJ had admitted she was okay with keeping the name JJ instead of changing back to Lydia.

"As much as I love the name my parents gave me, I wouldn't be where I am without JJ," she'd said. "It feels more wrong than right to give her up."

Price was wondering how she would feel becoming a Collins, but had decided to wait until after he proposed. Which he planned on doing in the near future. With the same ring that had belonged to her mother.

"I know I can't remember her, but I feel like Mom would have wanted JJ to have this," Josiah had told him when it had become evident to everyone just how much Price had fallen for JJ. He'd pulled him aside one Sunday dinner and handed the engagement ring over. "I'd like to keep Dad's ring, though, if you don't mind. Whether I wear it or pass it down to my kids, I'd like to hang on to him a bit longer."

Price had thought that was an idea that the late Ortiz parents would enjoy.

It also gave Riker an opening to pull him aside and officially give the father-in-law speech to him.

"You've seen her fight, you've seen her think, so I don't

have to tell you that you'll be sorry if you ever wrong her," Riker had said. "But, on the off chance that isn't enough, let me tell you that if you ever hurt that little girl of mine, you'll have to deal with me right after."

His words had been nothing but intimidating—and accepted.

Though, six months later when Riker would walk JJ down the aisle at their wedding, he'd be blubbering like a baby.

But now, sitting in his truck, Price's wandering thoughts wandered right into the hand he took in his.

"If you think this is a dream, then let me show you it isn't."

Price leaned over and kissed the woman he loved. He felt her smile into it. When he broke the kiss, he was smiling too.

"Satisfied now?" he asked.

JJ surprised him with a laugh and a shrug.

"I guess," she said. "Though, I wouldn't say no to you trying to convince me a little more later tonight."

Price let out a bite of laughter.

"That, I can do."

* * * * *